Light Can Be
Both Wave and Particle

Ellen Gilchrist lives in Fayetteville, Arkansas

Light Can Be
Both Wave and Particle

Ellen Gilchrist

faber and faber
LONDON · BOSTON

First published in the USA in 1989
by Little, Brown and Company, Boston
and simultaneously in Canada
by Little, Brown and Company (Canada) Limited
First published in Great Britain in 1990
by Faber and Faber Limited
3 Queen Square London WCIN 3AU
This paperback edition first published in 1991

Printed in England by Clays Ltd, St Ives plc

The author is grateful to the editors of the following publications
in whose pages some of the stories in this volume originally
appeared: *Cosmopolitan Magazine* for "Starlight Express";
London Daily News for "Blue Hills at Sundown"; and Albondocani Press
for "The Man Who Kicked Cancer's Ass" and "Blue Hills at Sundown".

Excerpt from "Me and Bobby McGee" by Kris Kristofferson and
Fred Foster. Copyright © 1969 Combine Music Corporation.
All rights controlled and administered by SBK Blackwood Music Inc.
All Rights Reserved. International Copyright Secured. Used by permission.

Excerpt from "Kiss on My List" by Janna Allen and Daryl Hall.
Copyright © 1980 Hot-Cha Music Co., Fust Buzza Music,
Unichappel Music Inc. All rights reserved. Used by permission.

A CIP record for this book is available from the British Library

ISBN 0-571-16166-9

For Dooley and Bunky, first line of defense.

"Not that anything I wrote about them is untrue, far from it. Yet when I wrote, the full facts were not at my disposal. The picture I drew was a provisional one, like the picture of a lost civilization deduced from a few fragmented vases, an inscribed tablet, an amulet, some human bones, a gold smiling death mask."

From *Clea,* by Lawrence Durrell

Contents

Rhoda

The Tree Fort

I HAVE BEEN HAUNTED lately by memories of Seymour, Indiana. A story in a magazine set me off and set me dreaming, of my brother, Dudley, and the fort, and the year he lost the eye. A fort made out of Christmas trees, piled four trees high, on the flat ground where the yard ran down to meet the alley. Dudley's pyramid, a memorial to the light in his left eye.

The first time I saw the fort was on a Saturday morning in January. I was coming home from my ballet lesson, walking up the alley from Sycamore Street, dragging my ballet shoes behind me by the laces, on the lookout for anything valuable anyone might have thrown away. I had found a hand-painted card shuffler in that alley once. It could happen again at any time.

I was almost home when I saw the activity in the yard. There were three boys, Dudley and Miles Pennington and Ronnie Breiner. They were standing beside a pile of Christmas trees. Dudley had his hands on his hips. He was wearing his jodhpurs and his hunting vest. His hair was as short as a marine recruit's. My father kept it cut that way to save him from vanity. Dudley stood in the middle of his friends, a young Douglas MacArthur, mulling over his problem. As I drew nearer I could see the Clifford twins coming down the side yard dragging another tree. It was Epiphany, the sixth of January, the day good Christians throw their trees away. What was Dudley up to and how had he once again hit upon an idea so wonderful, so startling in its power and simplicity, that it was certain to ruin my life for weeks?

"What are you doing?" I called out, as I crossed the victory garden and made for the pile of trees. "What's everyone doing?"

"We're building a fort," Dudley said. "Go in the house and get us some water and bring it out here if you want to help."

"Get your own hell damn water," I said, and went on by the trees. "Why are you building a fort?"

"To have a club. We're going to have a war with Billy Bob Robbins."

"How will we stack them up?" Ronnie Breiner asked. "I don't see what's going to keep them up."

"Just get them," Dudley answered. He was slouched over on one hip, wearing all seven of his lanyards. "We'll get them up. Get us some water, Shorty, if you want to help." He always called me Shorty. He got the idea from a gangster movie. I ignored him and went on into the house to put my ballet things away. From around the corner on the other side I could see Wayne Shorter and his friends dragging two more trees into the yard. It was eleven-thirty on a Saturday morning, right in the middle of a world war, and once again Dudley had found a way to ruin my life.

*　　*　　*

By noon they had a circle of trees piled four trees high and held together with clothes line and two-by-fours. Inside the circle was an enclosed space about as large as a bedroom. They filled that with old sleeping bags and a camouflage tarpaulin. I sat on the back steps and watched the activity. I was eating a sandwich and sucking a baby bottle filled with chocolate milk. My mother had a new baby and I could borrow his baby bottles anytime I wanted to and use them to suck chocolate milk. The milk picked up a wonderful flavor as it passed through the rubber nipple. I bit off a small piece so the milk would flow more easily. I knew they could see me drinking out of the bottle but I didn't care. It never occurred to me to stop doing something just because someone was looking at me.

They were dividing up into teams now. One team to hold the fort and the other to attack. Dudley's team would defend the fort. I see him now, standing on a ladder, sighting down across his arm with a wooden rifle, both eyes still in perfect working order, mowing down the invaders, then charging out in the forefront of his men, shooting as he ran. Coming to meet him from beside the French doors were Billy Bob and his horde of scrawny kids from the new development on the other side of Calvin Boulevard. I sucked my bottle. The January sun beat down on Seymour, Indiana. Inside my little plaid skirt and sweater my hot sweaty little body sucked down the rubber-flavored chocolate milk and watched the battle of the fort proceed.

When my father came home from the Air Corps base that afternoon he immediately took over rebuilding the fort. He made Dudley and Wayne take down all the two-by-fours and stack them up in a better configuration. "Those goddamn trees could fall on someone and hurt them," he said. "You boys are going to get me sued." Then Dudley and Wayne had to labor until dark shoring up the fort and making it safe.

He did not, however, seem to mind that every dead Christmas tree on Calvin Boulevard was piled up in our back yard killing the grass, and when mother mentioned it he told her to calm down and leave the boys alone. There's plenty of grass in the world, he told her, the grass can take care of itself. I had decided to stay out of it. I didn't even tell her that Billy Bob's regiment had trampled her roses as they pulled their tanks up from the alley for a surprise attack.

That night, tired as he was and with his hands red and raw from laboring on the fort in the January weather, Dudley made the first of the rubber guns. He fashioned it from pine, although later the guns would be made of finer woods, cypress and maple and persimmon and even walnut. He made the stock by whittling down a split two-by-four and sanding it for an hour. He was just beginning on the trigger mechanism when mother made him turn out the lights. At that time I was in the habit of sleeping in his room when I got scared. I would pay him three cents a night to sleep in his extra bed or five cents to sleep curled up on the foot of his bed. I was deathly afraid of the dark in those years. I feared the insides of closets and the space beneath my cherry four-poster bed and the goblins that get you if you don't watch out and angels coming for to carry you home and vampires and mummies and the holy ghost. I would wake from dreams and go running into my parents' room in the middle of the night when I slept alone. I was pathologically, deathly afraid of the dark, of night and shadow and the wages of sin. So I was sleeping in Dudley's extra bed when he turned the light back on and went back to work on the rubber gun. He added a carved handle and a trigger made out of a wooden clothespin and then dug around in a dresser drawer for a rubber band and used it to demonstrate for me how the trigger would release the band. "Of course, we'll have to make better things to shoot," he said. "We'll have to cut up old inner tubes."

"Will you make me one?" I asked. I felt very close to Dudley that night, watching him at his desk, risking a whipping to finish his work. He was brave, braver than I was in every way, and I loved him, with his thin face and his long thin arms and high intelligence quotient and his ability to stand up to and get along with our father. I had seen our father pull off his belt and beat Dudley in front of his friends and Dudley would never say a word. He took punishment like a man. He worked like a man. He was a man. I was safe in his room. No mummy or vampire would ever come in there. It was worth five cents to get a night's sleep without having to worry about the closets or underneath the beds.

"I might," he said. "If I have time."

"Will I get to be in the fort?"

"I doubt it, Shorty. You're a girl. Girls aren't supposed to be in everything."

"I'll make one of my own, then. Can I have part of the trees?" He shook his head and went back to work, enlarging the place on the stock where the clothespin would fit and lock in.

"I'm getting a diamond ring," I said and slipped back

down beneath the covers. I liked to keep my neck covered at all times when I was asleep. Even in Dudley's room you couldn't be too careful about vampires. "When Momma dies she's leaving me her ring."

"Go to sleep," he said, and held the gun up to the light to inspect it. "You're making too much noise. You're going to wake them up."

The fort became a permanent fixture in the back yard. The fort stayed. Winter progressed into spring. The Christmas trees turned brown and brittle and lost their needles and the needles were swept up and used to mulch the rose garden, which had been rebuilt by Dudley and his gang. All our roses bloomed that spring, American Beauties and Rosa Damascena, which dates back to the Crusades, and the dark red Henry Nevard and Rosa Alba, the white rose of York, and Persian Yellow and Fruehling's Gold and Maiden's Blush, our cutting of which had come to Indiana from Glen Allen, Mississippi, hand-delivered by our cousin, Laualee, who was a lieutenant in the navy.

The fort grew, taking up all the room between the back porch and the rose garden and the alley. The cedar and pine needles were reinforced by boards donated by boys from around the neighborhood. A tower was added and a permanent scaling ladder. Paths were worn along the sides of the house as invading forces charged down the hill. Later, the spring rains turned the paths into gullies.

The manufacture of rubber guns proceeded apace. The strips of rubber were of varying sizes, as Dudley experimented with different types of inner tubes. He would sit for hours in the evenings, sanding and polishing the stocks and handles, cutting old inner tubes into strips, sewing holsters from scraps of unbleached domestic and suiting samples.

March turned into April and April into May. The allies were winning the war in Europe. The clock in my second-grade classroom was the cruelest clock in the world. The days until the end of the school year seemed to last forever. At last my trunk was brought up from the basement and aired out and I began to fill it with T-shirts and socks and shorts and flashlight batteries. In June I was going to camp. I loved camp. I adored camp. I would have liked to go to camp all year. At camp I was the leader. At camp I had people sleeping around me every night. Without paying a single cent I had a whole room full of people to sleep with.

This year I was going to a new camp in Columbus, Ohio. Columbus Girls' Camp. A letter came with a sticker to put on my suitcase and another one for my trunk. I forgot about the fort. Who needed the hell damn fort? I was going off to Columbus Girls' Camp to row boats and swim in races and make lanyards and build campfires and sleep in a cabin with people all around me, far from the vampires and mummies and holy ghosts who inhabit real houses where families live.

So I was not there when he lost the eye. "The eye is a tiny balloon that grows at the front of the brain." So it said in a book I took home from the library. "The cells at the back are tuned to be sensitive to light, enabling us to see the world around us. The eye is so delicate that it has to be protected by a bony socket and eyelids to cover the window and a flow of tears to keep the window clean."

*   *   *

On the day he lost the eye, Dudley and Billy Bob and Miles and Ronnie were attacking as a tank corps. Wayne and Sam were inside the fort. The other boys were pushing wagons loaded with staves down from the back porch. There was an incline of about forty degrees, plenty good for accelerating wagon-tanks. Dudley was standing up in a wagon holding a loaded rubber gun and Miles was pushing him. Billy Bob was beside him in the other wagon. It was the tenth or twelfth or twentieth time they had run the wagons down the hill toward the fort. They were getting better and better at guiding them, but somehow or other this time Billy Bob's wagon ran into the side of Dudley's wagon and in the melee Dudley's rubber gun backfired and the thin band of old inner tube managed to elude the bony socket and the eyelid and dealt a blow to Dudley's eye. There goes my eye, I guess he said. It's a good thing it's on the left side. Anyway, there was blood, lots of blood. The German housekeeper held Dudley in her arms while Momma and Sam and Wayne ran for Doctor Shorter, and later that night, when the bleeding wouldn't stop, they took him to the doctors at the Air Corps base and the next day the Air Corps flew him to Memphis to an eye surgeon.

It took all summer to heal. It was September before Dudley came home with his eye still swathed in bandages.

When the bandages came off he could see light and dark and distinguish shapes, but nothing more. There were blood clots behind the iris, and the doctors were afraid to operate for fear it would set up sympathetic problems with the good eye. That's all we talked about from then on. Dudley's good eye. How to protect his good eye. How never to take chances with his good eye. How his good eye was doing. Thank God for his good eye. Pray for his good eye.

While Dudley was in Memphis the fort had fallen into disrepair. Children from all over the neighborhood came and inspected it and told each other about the tank battle. An aura of mystery and danger hung around the circle of trees, timeless, Druidic, threatening. I never went near the place. I knew bad karma when I felt it. The sleeping bags were in there rotting away but I didn't go in and drag them out. By the time Mother got home from Memphis they were filled with ants and had to be pitched out for the garbage-men.

Dudley had a strange relationship with the fort after he returned from Memphis. I remember him standing there with his big black patch on his eye, wearing his brown and white tweed knickers, his hands on his hips, looking at the fort, not defeated or scared or really puzzled even. Just standing there looking it over.

Then one day the following spring, after D-Day, when the pressure was letting up all over the United States and men could go back to ruining the lives of their children, my father looked up over his breakfast oatmeal and said, "Son, today we are going to have to get rid of those trees. Your mother wants the grass to grow back before the owners of this house return."

"They will think we are white trash," my mother added. She was poaching eggs in a black skillet, a little blue and white apron over her blue shirtwaist dress. I was sitting in the corner of the breakfast nook pulling on my hair to make it grow.

"Let's clear them out," my father went on. "Get Wayne and Billy Bob and let them help."

"I'm not helping," I said. "It's not my damn old fort."

"I'm going to wash your mouth out with soap," my mother put in. "Dudley, please do something about her."

"No one expects you to help," my brother said.

"No one expects you to do a thing," my father added. "You are a very selfish little girl."

I slid down under the table and climbed out and stood beside my mother. I didn't care what they thought. As soon as the war was over I was going to be a movie star. When I got to Hollywood I would probably never even write to them again. Dudley looked at me out of his good eye. He looked so thin and sad. I guess he was thinking about how terrible it was going to feel to have to drag all those prickly trees back to the alley and then rake up the yard and even then get yelled at and probably get a whipping before the day was out. I'm glad Daddy doesn't like me, I was thinking. The more he likes you, the more trouble you are in.

"Clean up your room," someone called after me but it was too late. I was through the dining room and past the green chair and out the door. I could feel the morning calling from the front yard and I ran on out and headed down Calvin Boulevard to see what I could find to do.

It was a glamorous spring day. The gold star in Mrs. Allen's window gleamed in the light. The apple trees in the Hancock's yard had burst into bloom. Elsie Carter came riding down the boulevard carrying her sack of *Saturday Evening Post*s. One of my molars was about to fall out. I could taste the wonderful thin, salty taste of blood. I was eight years old. In five years darker blood would pour out from in between my legs and all things would be changed. For now, I was pure energy, clear light, morally neutral, soft and violent and almost perfect. I had two good eyes and two good ears and two arms and two legs. If bugs got inside of me, my blood boiled and ate them up. If I cut myself, my blood rushed in and sewed me back together. If a tooth fell out, another one came in. The sunlight fell between the branches of the trees. It was Saturday. I had nothing to do and nowhere to go and I didn't have to do a thing I didn't want to do and it would be a long time before things darkened and turned to night.

The Time Capsule

NINETEEN HUNDRED AND FORTY-FOUR. In a year the Japanese would surrender but Rhoda did not know that yet. She was worried sick about the Japanese. Forty years later she would smell a fig tree beside a bakery and remember how her swing looked down on fig trees during those fateful years while she waited to see who would win the war.

It was not an ordinary swing. It was the tallest backyard swing in Seymour, Indiana, thirty feet high, constructed of tall pine uprights sunk in concrete shoes. The rope was an inch thick. There was a seat of solid pine fitted into the rope by hundreds of hours of Rhoda's relentless swinging. She could swing holding a doll or a sandwich. She could swing standing up or sitting down. She could swing so high the ropes snapped at the top. Every morning she would come down the back stairs and across the yard and get in and take off. Off we go, she would be singing. Into the wild blue yonder. Climbing high into the sky.

One morning in August she was swinging more

slowly than usual because she was thinking about fate. Anything could happen to anyone at any time. That much was clear. You could be on the losing side of a war. You could fall in love and get married. Hollywood could come and get you for a movie star. Your mother could die and leave you her rings. You could die.

Rhoda stopped the swing. She dragged her toes in the dirt. No, she would never die. She was not the type. It was probably a lie like everything else they told you. She smelled her arms. They smelled alive. She lifted her head. She tossed her hair. To hell with death, damn it all to goddamn hell. She concentrated on the fig tree above the sandpile. Let them come with death. She would smash them in the face. She would tie them to a tree and beat them with willow whips and jump in her plane and take off for the island where her mother waited. She dug her toes deeper in the soft, loose dirt beneath the swing. Red dirt, as red as blood, not dark like dirt in the Delta, like black dirt and black skin and rivers. This was the red dirt of Indiana, where they had to live because a war was going on. This was the war and everyone must do their part. She leaned far out of the swing until the ropes cut into her arms. She dug her toes into the dirt until her sandals were covered with it. Then she pushed back off into the sky. She pumped with her arms and legs. She went higher and higher, this time she would go forever, this time she would flip the swing over the uprights and come plummeting down.

It had been a bad summer. First Gena's sister told her blood was going to come out from in between her legs one week out of every four. There was nothing she could do about it. No one was excluded. Then her father took her and her mother to see *The Outlaw* with Jane Russell and made them leave at the part where Jane was warming her boyfriend's body in the haystack. "I'll keep you warm," Jane was saying. "I'll save you." Big Dudley had grabbed them up and dragged them out of the theater. He was furious with Ariane for exposing Rhoda to filth.

But the main thing was the newsreel. The news from the Pacific did not look good. Americans were dying on every island. It was possible they would lose the war. Rhoda stopped the swing. It was time to make a time capsule. She must leave a record so future generations would know she had been here. She got out of the swing and dusted off her dress and went into the kitchen. Mrs. Dustin was there, the German lady who worked for the Mannings now that they were someplace where there weren't any black people. Mrs. Dustin wasn't nice like black people. She only worked for them because she had to. She didn't even love them. "Stay out of the refrigerator," she said now. "Your mother doesn't want you eating between meals."

"I need this matchbox," Rhoda said. She took it off the stove and dumped the matches on the table.

"Don't take that," Mrs. Dustin began, but it was too late. Rhoda was out the door, the sash of her pinafore trailing behind her. She was dressed up today, wearing a green and white checked dress and an organdy pinafore. She had a green velvet ribbon tied around her wrist to ward off the story of the blood coming out down there. Down there, down there, down there. Do not put anything down there. Do not stick anything inside yourself down there. Wash your hands before you touch yourself down there. There was a wonderful quality to her mother's voice when she talked of it, scary and worried. Now, on top of everything else, there was this god-damn story about the blood. "It happens to every single girl," Gena's sister had said. "No one can escape it. You can never go swimming again. You have to have this big lump of absorbent cotton between your legs and it hurts so much you have to go to bed." The minute Rhoda got home she had fallen down on her knees beside her bed to beg God not to let it happen to her. As usual there was no answer, so she got up and went to find her mother. "Why would Gena's sister tell you such a thing? I can't believe she told you something like that," Rhoda's mother said.

"Then it's true?"

"No, it's not exactly true. It will be a long time before it happens to you and it doesn't hurt. It's God's way of making us able to have babies."

"Blood comes out from in between your legs?"

"Yes, but not for a long time. Rhoda, you are just a little girl. You don't have to worry about this yet."

"I hate God. I hate His guts. That's just like Him to think up something like that." She left the room. When she got to the door she called back across her shoulder, "I wouldn't have your old God for all the tea in China. I think He looks like hell in that old robe."

That was the day before. Today Rhoda was on the offensive where fate was concerned. She went down the back stairs, holding the matchbox in her hand, and up on a rise to a place where she had been digging a foxhole the year before. She had abandoned the project because of a book she read about a little girl who went blind from staring at the sun. She had stayed inside for weeks after she read it. The shovel was still there. She picked it up and began to dig. Her hands were so strong and so valuable. Her mother was a princess, her father was a king, she was so wonderful and valuable. She must never die or be lost in any way. She dug as fast as she could, thinking of things that must go into the capsule. A picture of herself, the picture she sent to Margaret O'Brien after seeing *Journey for Margaret.* A man had left his luggage in London so that Margaret could get on the plane and fly to safety. I would do it, Rhoda decided. I would leave all my worldly goods behind to save a little girl. She dug awhile longer, imagining it. Then she dropped the shovel and took the matchbox inside to fill it up. She walked through the French doors and into the living room of the high-ceilinged stucco house someone in Seymour, Indiana had copied from a picture of a French château they found in a magazine.

Rhoda took down the photograph album from a shelf and dusted it off with her skirt and found the photograph she wanted. It was a picture of herself sitting on a Persian rug in a white dress. Yes, it would do to carry her into the future. She tore it out of the book and sat down at her mother's desk to write the message.

My name is Rhoda Katherine Manning. I weigh 82. We are in a war. They might come at any minute. I have auburn hair and brown eyes. I was born on a plantation in the Delta and as soon as the war is over I'll be going back. Mrs. Allen's son died in the war. She has a gold star in the window and I go and visit her quite frequently. The pope wouldn't let her be my brother's godmother. She isn't allowed to go inside our church. No one tells me what to do. I am just like my father.

Well, I see I am running out of paper. When you find this think of me. It is summer and the sun is shining and everything is fine around here so far. I will include my fingerprints.

> *Yours truly,*
> *Rhoda Manning*

She looked up from her writing, stuck her thumbs in the inkwell, added her thumbprints, blew the ink dry, then rolled the message up into a scroll. She went into the kitchen, got some wax paper, covered the scroll with it and added a rubber band. Then she went up to her room to see what she could find to put in the capsule. She chose a picture of Alan Ladd, a string of beads, three pennies and an empty perfume bottle. She arranged the things neatly in the matchbox and pushed the cover shut. There. That should give them a pretty good idea of what Seymour, Indiana was like in nineteen forty-four. She marched back out to the garden and began to dig again. The smell of the earth came up to meet her, cold and fresh. A robin called. A breeze touched her face. It was perfect. Rhoda sat back upon her heels and thought about the inside of the earth, how many things are buried there. Valuable things you could find, things you could eat. She put her face in her hands, sank back deeper on her heels, thinking of her victory garden, how small and tough the carrots were, what a disappointment. Dudley had laughed at her carrots. He said a rabbit wouldn't eat the carrots that came up in her patch. Dudley. Why did they like him so much? Why was he so good? Why did he always get away with murder? Why did he have all the friends?

He was coming across the yard toward her now, wearing his jodhpurs and his riding boots. He stopped, one hip cocked out, his black patch over his injured eye.

"Get out of here," she said. "I'm doing something."

"Let me see."

"It's a time capsule." She handed over the matchbox. He opened it and looked inside.

"You ought to put your scout pin in. There ought to be something about the scouts."

"Well, I don't have anything else. That's all that's going in."

"This is going to rot. You ought to get a tin box."

"Just mind your own business."

"I'd use tin if I was you. You want me to get you a can?" He was getting his hooded look. Rhoda grew wary. There were no meaningless encounters between Rhoda and Dudley. Every word and gesture was charged with meaning and intent. There was no meager stuff here. It was the world they were fighting for.

"Just mind your own beeswax," she said. "Just leave me alone." He backed off. He actually walked away. Turned his back and walked away. Rhoda dug a few more inches in the ground, stuffed the box in the hole and covered it with dirt. Then she got up and went into the house to see what he was doing.

He was in his room with the door shut. There was the sound of shuffling, the sound of muffled voices, muffled laughter. Rhoda pressed her ear to the door. Laughter again. It was Cody Wainwright. They were doing something. They were talking about their secret things. She would use the hidden passageway behind the stairs. They would never know she was there. She could stay there for hours without a sound, hot and close in the little alcove behind his room.

She climbed down through the small door and into the crawl space between the dormers, walking on the two-by-fours. She sat down on the crossbeams. She prepared to listen. Nothing was going on. They weren't talking. They weren't saying anything. Someone laughed. It was Dudley. Yes, it was Dudley laughing. Cody laughed back. Silence. Only silence. They turned the radio on. It was hot. Before long she would breathe up all the air. She would die back here and no one would ever find her. She got up and beat on the wall of his room. "I hear you in there. I can hear every word you're saying. I heard everything you said." Then she climbed back out the door and turned around to face them. "I heard you," she said. "If you hit me I'll tell her everything you said."

"You're a nasty bad little girl," Dudley said. "You are as bad as anyone gets to be."

"Let's take her with us to the sweetshop," Cody said. "Let's get her a lemonade."

"She's been out in the yard making a time capsule with her picture in it." Dudley laughed and turned his back on her. "That's how much she likes herself. She thinks someone's going to be interested in her after she's dead." He laughed again, a dark vicious laugh, and took his friend's arm and left her there.

A week later Rhoda's father came home one afternoon and announced that they were moving to Terre Haute, Indiana, to build another airport. They had one week to pack up and be there. The War Department was going to build the biggest airport in Indiana and get this goddamn war over with. They were going to live in a famous writer's house, a writer named Virginia Sorensen.

The writer had a little girl just Rhoda's age and Rhoda would live in this child's room. They must hurry and put everything in storage. The war was heating up. There must be more airports, more pilots, more planes. Everyone must pitch in and do their share. They must tighten their belts, pack the boxes, get on the move.

Dudley began to cry. He was afraid to go to a different school so soon after he lost his eye. Rhoda's mother put her arms around him and cried too. Only Rhoda and her father did not cry. Only Rhoda and her father had enough sense to win a war. Rhoda took some boxes up to her room and began to throw things into them, singing as she worked. "Over hill, over dale, as we hit the dusty trail. And those caissons go rolling along. . . ." She threw in her movie star pictures and her music box and her false fingernail set and her Kiddie Kurlers and her hot water bottle. She threw in her books and started on her dresser drawers. All her nice white socks. The pair of ecru rayon pants her mother wouldn't let her wear because they were tacky. She held them up to the light. There were stripes of ecru silk. She threw them in and finished off the drawer. A rumpled sheet of white tissue paper was in the bottom. She folded it and left it in the drawer. Jimmy got up out of a corner and came and stood by the boxes. He was her imaginary playmate. He had come to live with her when she was four, when her mother was in the hospital. He had stayed with her all that long year. He had sat with her on the fire escape of the apartment in Louisville, Kentucky, waiting for the bread man to come and bring the bread with the picture of the Seven Dwarfs. Rhoda hadn't seen him in a long time. Now he was here, wearing his gray suit and white shirt and black tie, wearing his cynical look. "Well,

I see we're moving again," he said. "I hope you don't get a bad teacher like you did last time. I'll never forget that day."

Rhoda stopped packing. She sat down on the bed. All her courage disappeared. The day she had come to Seymour to the new school, a fat, blond teacher had put her in the bad reading group. THE LOWER GROUP. Rhoda Katherine Manning, the best reader in the world, sitting in the back of the room. She had sat there all day until they found out she could read. "It could happen again," Jimmy said. "Go find her. Make sure she knows. Go find her right now. Get it settled."

Rhoda found her mother in the bathroom packing the iodine and alcohol and Mercurochrome and hydrogen peroxide. "If you put me in a school that puts me in a dumb reading class I will kill myself. You had better be sure they don't do that."

"Oh, darling." Her mother closed the bathroom cabinet and sat down on the edge of the tub. "I'm so sorry. So sorry about everything. I'm doing all I can. I'm doing everything I know how to do."

"Just be sure about the school."

"I will. I promise I will. I'll go with you the first day and take your test scores. I'll talk to the teacher before you go there. Nothing will happen. I promise you. You're going to live in a writer's house, honey. She wrote *A Little Lower Than the Angels*. We'll get all her books and read them. It will be an adventure. We must be brave, darling, we're in a war."

"I know. You already told me that. How big a room?"

"Plenty big. Your father said it had a blackboard. And Rhoda, don't worry about the school. I will never let that happen to you again."

"It better not."

"It won't. I promise you. Things can't be perfect right now, honey. We have to get this war over. Our men are dying over there. We have to save as many as we can." As soon as she said it Ariane regretted the words. It was not good to say dead or death to Rhoda. The child backed up and moved into the corner.

"What does it mean to die? What happens to you?" Rhoda was near the sink. She could smell the alcohol and the Mercurochrome. It smelled like the hospital where she had had her tonsils out the year before. They had strapped her to a table and put a mask on her face and dripped sleeping gas on it. Her mother and father were in the hall. Nuns were all around her, holding her down. There was nothing she could do. Her life was in the hands of nuns and strangers. Death will be like that, Rhoda thought. They will hold you down and drip poison in your nose and there will be nothing you can do and your mother will be out in the hall. She refused her mother's hands. "I can't stand to die," she screamed. "I hate God. I hate it all so much. I won't do it. They can't make me do it. They won't get me. I won't hold still. I won't go in there. Go to goddamn hell, that's what I'm going to tell them. You won't make me die, you goddam old God, to hell with you."

Her mother had her now. Her mother had her in her arms. "It isn't like that, honey. People you love are up there waiting for you. You can be with Jesus. He died to give us everlasting life. He frees us from death."

"That's a lie. None of it is true. Nothing you ever tell me is true." Her mother dropped her arms. She sighed a long deep sigh. Rhoda was too much. Too smart for her own good. Too wild, too crazy, too hard to manage or control. She was a long way from the sweet little redheaded girl Ariane had ordered from Jesus. Thinking of Jesus, Ariane remembered her duty. She fought back. "You just calm down, young lady. You just stop all that talk right this minute."

"Make sure about the school," Rhoda said and made her exit. She went into the hall and found Jimmy waiting at the top of the stairs. She took his arm and started down. "Let's go dig up the time capsule," she said. "I might need that picture where I'm going." She stamped down the wooden stairs, making as much noise as she could on every stair, stamp, stamp, stamp, back in control with Jimmy by her side. She lifted her head and began to sing. "I'm happy when I'm hiking. Off the beaten track. I'm happy when I'm hiking. Pack upon my back. With a right good friend, to the journey's end. Ten, twenty, thirty, forty, fifty miles a day. Tramp, tramp, tramp, tramp."

"The name of the pack is life or death," Jimmy muttered. "Therefore, let's keep moving."

Some Blue Hills
at Sundown

IT WAS THE LAST TIME Rhoda would ever see Bob Rosen
in her life. Perhaps she knew that the whole time she
was driving to meet him, the long drive through the
November fields, down the long narrow state of Kentucky, driving due west, then across the Ohio River and
up into the flat-topped hills of Southern Illinois.

If it had been any other time in her life or any other
boyfriend she would have been stopping every fifty
miles to look at herself in the mirror or spray her wrists
with perfume or smooth the wrinkles from her skirt. As
it was she drove steadily up into the hills with the
lengthening shadows all around her. She didn't glance
at her watch, didn't worry about the time. He would be
there when she got there, waiting at the old corrugated
building where he worked on his car, the radio playing,
his cat sitting on a shelf by the Tune Oil, watching.
Nothing would have changed. Only she was two months
older and he was two months older and there had been
another operation. When he got home from the hospital he had called her and said, "Come on if you can. I'll
be here the rest of the semester. Come if you want to.

Just let me know." So she had told her mother and father that if they didn't let her go she would kill herself and they believed her, so caught up in their terrible triangle and half-broken marriage and tears and lies and sadness that they couldn't fight with her that year. Her mother tried to stop it.

"Don't give her a car to go up there and see that college boy," her mother said. "Don't you dare do that, Dudley. I will leave you if you do."

So her father had loaned her the new Cadillac, six thousand dollars' worth of brand-new car, a fortune of a car in nineteen fifty-three, and she had driven up to Southern Illinois to see Bob Rosen and tell him that she loved him. No, just to see him and look at his face. No, to watch him work on his car. No, to smell the kind soft whiteness of his cheeks. To see him before he died. Untold madness of the dark hour. "Now by this moon, before this moon shall wane, I shall be dead or I shall be with you."

He was waiting for her. Not working on the car. Not even inside the building. Standing outside on the street, leaning against the building, smoking a cigarette and waiting. One foot on top of the other foot, his soft gray trousers loose around the ankles, his soft white skin, his tall lanky body fighting every minute for its life.

"Hello," he said. "I'm glad to see you. Let me see this goddamn car. Where did you get this car? My God, that's some car."

"He's getting rich. Just like he said he would. Who cares. I hate it there. There isn't anything to do. No one to talk to. I think about you all the time." He slid into the driver's seat and turned around and took her into his arms. It was the first time in two months that she had been happy. Now, suddenly, it seemed as if this moment would be enough to last forever, would make up for all the time that would follow.

"I ought to just turn around and go home now," she said. "I guess I just wanted to make sure you were real."

"It wouldn't be a good idea to get in the habit of loving me. I shouldn't have let you come up here."

"I asked to come."

"So you did. Well, look here. Let's go to the sweetshop and get a sandwich and see who's there. I'll bet you haven't eaten all day."

"I don't want to eat anything." She pulled away. "I want to do it. You said you'd do it to me. You promised me. You swore you would."

"When did I do that?"

"You know."

"Rhoda, Rhoda, Rhoda. Jesus. Exactly where did you envision this deflowering taking place?"

"In the car, I guess. Or anywhere. Where do people go?"

"I don't go anywhere with sixteen-year-old girls. I'd go to jail, that's where I'd go. Come here." He pulled her across his legs and kissed her again, then turned around toward the steering wheel and turned on the ignition. "Talk while I drive. I'll take you out to the roadside park. It's completely dark out there. You can see a thousand stars. Remember that night Doc Stanford was here from Louisville and we played music out there? You were having that goddamn slumber party and I had to take all your goddamn friends to get you out of the house. My friends still haven't let me stop hearing about that. That cousin of yours from Mississippi was there. Do you remember that night?"

"You won't do it?"

"Hell, no, I won't do it. But I want to. If it gives you

any satisfaction you'd better believe I want to." They were cruising very slowly down a dark street that led upward through a field of poplars. There was one streetlight at the very top of the deserted street. "I drive by your house every now and then. It seemes like the whole street died when your family left. Everyone misses you. So your father's doing well?"

"They're getting a divorce. He's having an affair and my mother acts like she's crazy. That's why I got to come. They're too busy to care what I do. They sent Dudley off to a boys' school and next year I'm going to Virginia. I'll never get to come back here. If we don't do it tonight, we never will. That's what's going to happen, isn't it?"

"No, we are going to the sweetshop and get a malt and a ham sandwich and see who's there. Then I'm going to take you over to the Buchanans' house where you're supposed to be before someone calls out the state cops. Did you call and tell them you're in town?"

"No, they don't even know I'm coming. No one knows but Augusta. And Jane Anne. She had to tell Jane Anne." He shook his head and pulled her very close to him. She was so close to him she could feel him breathe. I'm like a pet dog to him, she decided. I'm just some little kid he's nice to. He doesn't even listen to what I say. What does he want me here for? He doesn't need me for a thing. It was dark all around them now, the strange quiet weekend dark of small midwestern towns in the innocent years of the nineteen fifties. Rhoda shuddered. It was so exciting. So terrible and sad and exciting, so stifled and sad and terrible and real. This is really happening, she was thinking. This feeling, this loving him more than anything in the world and in a second it will be over. It ends as it happens and it will never be again in any way, never happen again or stop happening. It is so thick, so tight around me. I think this is what those old fairy tales meant. This is how those old stories always made me feel.

"I want you to know something," he said. He had stopped the car. "I want you to know that I would have made love to you if I had been well. If you had been older and I had been well and things had been different. You are a wonderful girl, Rhoda. A blessing I got handed that I can't ever figure out. DeLisle loves you. You know that? He asks me about you all the time. He says he can't figure out what I did to deserve you writing me letters all the time."

"I don't want to talk about DeLisle."

"I'm taking you to the sweetshop now." He put the brake on the car and kissed her for a very long time underneath the streetlight. Their shadows were all around them and the wind moved the light and made the street alive with shadows and they held each other while the wind blew the light everywhere and her fingers found the scars on his neck and behind his ear and caressed them and there was nothing else to say or nothing else to do and they expanded and took in the sadness and shared it.

After a while he started the car and they went to the sweetshop and ate ham sandwiches and talked to people and then drove over to the Buchanans' house and he left her there and walked the six blocks home with his hands in his pockets. He was counting the months he might live. He thought it would be twenty-four but it turned out to be a lifetime after all.

Nora Jane

The Starlight Express

NORA JANE was seven months pregnant when Sandy disappeared again. *Dear Baby,* the note said. *I can't take it. Here's all the money that is left. Don't get mad if you can help it. I love you, Sandy.*

She folded up the note and put it in a drawer. Then she made up the bed. Then she went outside and walked along the water's edge. At least we are living on the water, she was thinking. I always get lucky about things like that. Well, I know one thing. I'm going to have these babies no matter what I have to do and I'm going to keep them alive. They won't die on me or get drunk or take cocaine. Freddy was right. A decent home is the best thing.

Nora Jane was on a beach fifty miles south of San Francisco, beside a little stucco house Sandy's old employer had been renting them for next to nothing. Nora Jane had never liked living in that house. Still, it was on the ocean.

The ocean spread out before her now, gray and dark, breaking against the boulders where it turned into a little cove. There were places where people had been making fires. Nora Jane began to pick up all the litter she could find and put it in a pile beside a firesite. She walked around for half an hour picking up cans and barrettes and half-burned pieces of cardboard and piled them up beside a boulder. Then she went back to the house and got some charcoal lighter and a match and lit the mess and watched it burn. It was the middle of October. December the fifteenth was only two months away. I could go to Freddy, she was thinking. He will always love me and forgive me anything. But what will it do to him? Do I have a right to get around him so he'll only love me more? This was a question Nora Jane was always asking herself about Freddy Harwood. Now she asked it once again.

A cold wind was blowing off the ocean. She picked up a piece of driftwood and added it to the fire. She sank down upon the sand. She was carrying ten pounds of babies but she moved as gracefully as ever. She wiggled around until her back was against the boulder, sitting up very straight, not giving in to the cold or the wind. I'm one of those people that could go to the Himalayas, she decided. Because I never give in to cold. If you hunch over it will get you.

Freddy Harwood stood on the porch of his half-finished house, deep in the woods outside of Willets, California, and thought about Nora Jane. He was thinking about her voice, trying to remember how it sounded when she said his name. If I could remember that sound, he decided. If I could remember what she said that first night it would be enough. If that's all I get it will have to do.

He looked deep into the woods, past the madrone

where once he had seen a bobcat come walking ou
lets. at the place where the trees ended and the
huge yellow cat with a muff around its
thought. So, there I go about the afternoon called
minds me of her or it doesn't remind me either re-
everything reminds me of her. What good does it do to
have six million dollars and two houses and a bookstore
if I'm in love with Nora Jane? Freddy left his bobcat
lookout and walked around the side of the house toward the road. A man was hurrying up the path.

It was his neighbor, Sam Lyons, who lived a few miles
away up an impassable road. Freddy waved and went to
meet him. He's coming to tell me she's dead, he decided.
She died in childbirth in the hands of a midwife in
Chinatown and I'm supposed to go on living after that.
"What's happening?" he called out. "What's going on?"

"You got a call," Sam said. "Your girlfriend's coming
on the train. I'm getting tired of this, Harwood. You get
yourself a phone. That's twice this week. *Two calls in one
week!*"

In a small neat room near the Berkeley campus a young
Chinese geneticist named Lin Tan Sing packed a
change of clothes and his toilet articles, left a note for
himself about some things to do when he returned, and
walked out into the beautiful fall day. He had been sav-
ing his money for a vacation and today was the day it
began. As soon as he finished work that afternoon he
would ride the subway to the train station and get on

Starlight Express and travel ...ng
coast to Puget Sound ...will look at
eyes have gone to ... Perhaps the train
ow I will go ou...
nd. People ...ean. There will be stories in
e will le... off ... Young Chinese scientist saves many
...aring rescues. President of United States invites
...Chinese scientist to live in White House and tutor
...en of politicians. Young Chinese scientist adopted
...ealthy man whose life he saves in train wreck. I am
...y a humble scientist trying to unravel genetic code,
...ung Chinese scientist tells reporters. Did not mean to
...e hero. Do not know what came over me. I pushed on
fallen car and great strength came to me when it was
least expected.

Lin Tan entered the Berkeley campus and strolled
along a sidewalk leading to the student union. Students
were all around. A man in black was playing a piano
beneath a tree. The sky was clear with only a few clouds
to the west. The Starlight Express, Lin Tan was thinking. All Plexiglas across the top. Stars rolling by while I
am inside with something nice to drink. Who knows?
Perhaps I will find a girl on the train who wishes to talk
with me. I will tell her all things scientific and also of
poetry. I will tell her the poetry of my country and also
of England. Lin Tan folded his hands before him as he
walked, already he was on the train, speeding up the
California coast telling some dazzling blonde the story
of his life and all about his work. Lin Tan worked at
night in the lab of the Berkeley Women's Clinic. He did
chemical analyses on the fluid removed during am-

niocentesis. So far he had made only one mistake in his work. One time a test had to be repeated because he knocked a petri dish off the table with his sleeve. Except for that his results had proved correct in every single instance. No one else in the lab had such a record. Because of this Lin Tan always kept his head politely bowed in the halls and was extra-nice to the other technicians and generous with advice and help. He had a fellowship in the graduate program in biology and he had this easy part-time job and his sister, Jade Tan Sing, was coming in six months to join him. Only one thing was lacking in Lin Tan's life and that was a girlfriend. He had what he considered a flaw in his character and wished to be in love with a Western girl with blond hair. It was only fate, the *I Ching* assured him. A fateful flaw that would cause disaster and ruin but not of his own doing and therefore nothing to worry about.

On this train, he was thinking, I will sit up straight and hold my head high. If she asks where I come from I will say Shanghai or Hong Kong as it is difficult for them to picture village life in China without thinking of rice paddies. I am a businessman, I will say, and have only taken time off to learn science. No, I will say only the truth so she may gaze into my eyes and be at peace. I will buy you jewels and perfume, I will tell her. Robes with silken dragons eating the moon, many pearls. Shoes with flowers embroidered on them for every minute of the day. Look out the Plexiglas ceiling at the stars. They are whirling by and so are we even when we are off the train.

Nora Jane bought her ticket and went outside to get some air while she waited for the train. She was wearing a long gray sweatshirt with a black leather belt riding on top of the twins. On her legs were bright yellow tights and yellow ballet shoes. A yellow and white scarf was tied around her black curls. She looked just about as wonderful as someone carrying ten pounds of babies could ever look in the world. She was deserted and unwed and on her way to find a man whose heart she had broken only four months before and she should have been in a terrible mood but she couldn't work up much enthusiasm for despair. Whatever chemicals Tammili and Lydia were pumping into her bloodstream were working nicely to keep Nora Jane in a good mood. She stood outside the train station watching a line of cirrus clouds chugging along the horizon, thinking about the outfits she would buy for her babies as soon as they were born. Nora Jane loved clothes. She couldn't wait until she had three people to dress instead of only one. All her life she had wanted to be able to wear all her favorite colors at one time. Now she would have her chance. She could just see herself walking into a drugstore holding her little girls by the hand. Tammili would be wearing blue. Lydia would be wearing red or pink. Nora Jane would have on peach or mauve or her old standby, yellow. Unless that was too many primaries on one day. I'll start singing, she decided. That way I can work at night while they're asleep. I have to have some money of my own. I don't want anyone supporting us. When I go shopping and buy stuff I don't want anybody saying why did you get this stuff and you didn't need that shirt and so forth. As soon as they're born I'll be able to work and make some money. Nieman said I could sing anyplace in San Francisco. Nieman should know. After all, he writes for the newspaper. If they don't like it then I'll just get a job in a day-care center like I meant to last fall. I'll do whatever I have to do.

A whistle blew. Nora Jane walked back down the concrete stairs. "Starlight Express," a black voice was calling out. "Get on board for the long haul to Washington State. Don't go if you're scared of stars. Stars all the way to Marin, San Rafael, Petaluma, and Sebastapol. Stars all the way to Portland, Oregon, and Seattle, Washington. Stars to Alaska and points north. Stars to the North Pole. Get on board this train. . . ."

Nora Jane threw her backpack over her shoulder and ran for the train. Lin Tan caught a glimpse of her yellow stockings and reminded himself not to completely rule out black hair in his search for happiness.

Freddy Harwood was straightening up his house. He moved the wooden table holding his jigsaw puzzle of the suspended whale from the Museum of Natural History. He watered his paper-white narcissus. He got a broom out of a closet and began to sweep the floor. He found a column Nieman did about *My Dinner with André* and leaned on the broom reading it. It was two o'clock in the afternoon and there was no reason to leave for the station before five. They aren't my babies, he reminded himself. She's having someone else's babies and they aren't mine and I don't want them anyway. Why do I want her at all? Because I like to talk to her, that's why. I like to talk to her more than anyone in the world. That's that. It's my business. Mine and only mine. I like to look at her and I like to talk to her. Jesus Christ! Could I have a maid? I mean would it violate every tenet if I had a maid once a week?

He threw the broom into a closet and pulled on his

boots and walked out into the yard to look for the bob-cat.

The house Freddy was stamping out of was a structure he had been building on and off for years. It was in Mendocino County near the town of Willets and could only be reached by a long winding uphill road that became impassable when it rained. Actually, it was impassable when it didn't rain but Freddy and his lone neighbor put their four-wheel jeeps in gear and pretended the rock-covered path was a road. Sometimes it even looked like a road, from the right angle and if several trips had been made in a single spell of dry weather.

The house sat on high ground and had several amazing views. To the west lay the coastal ranges of northern California. To the east the state game refuge of the Mendocino National Forest. In any direction were spruce trees and Douglas fir and Northern pine. Freddy had bought the place with the first money he ever earned. That was years ago, during the time when he stopped speaking to his family and smoked dope all day and worked as a chimney sweep. He had lived in a van and saved twelve thousand dollars. Then he had driven up the California coast until he found Douglas fir on land with no roads leading to it. He bought as much as twelve thousand dollars would buy. Two acres, almost three. Then he set up a tent and started building. He built a cistern to catch water and laid pipes to carry it to where the kitchen would later be. He leveled the land and poured a concrete foundation and marked off rooms and hauled stones for a fireplace. He planted fruit trees and a vineyard and put in root plants and an herb garden for medical emergencies. He had been working on the house off and on for twenty-three years. The house was as much a part of Freddy Harwood as his skin. When he was away from Willets for long stretches of time, he thought about the house every day, the red sun of early morning and the redder sun of sundown. The eyes of the bobcat in the woods, the endless lines of mountains in the distance. The taste of the air and the taste of the water. His body sleeping in peace in his own invention.

Now she's ruined my house for me, he was thinking, leaning against the madrone tree while he waited for the bobcat. She's slept in all the rooms and sat on the chairs and touched the furniture. She's used all the forks and spoons and moved the table. I'm putting it back where it goes today. Well, let her come up here and beg for mercy. I don't care. I'll give it to her. Let her cry her dumb little Roman Catholic heart out. I guess she looks like hell. I bet she's as big as a house. Well, shit, not that again.

He turned toward the house. A redbird was throwing itself against the windows. Bird in the house means bad luck. Well, don't let it get in. I'll have to put some screens on those windows. Ruin the light.

The house was very tall with many windows. It was a house a child might draw, tall and thin. Inside were six rooms, or areas, filled with books and mattresses and lamps and tables. Everything was white or black or brown or gray. Freddy had made all the furniture himself except for two chairs by Mies Van Der Rohe. A closet held all of Buiji Dalton's pottery in case she should come to visit. A shelf held Nieman's books. On a peg behind the bathroom door was Nora Jane's yellow silk kimono.

When she comes, Freddy was saying to himself as he trudged back up the hill to do something about the bird, I won't say a word about anything. I'll just act like everything is normal. Sam came over and said you'd be on the train and it was getting into Fort Bragg at eight and would I meet you. Well, great. I mean, what brought you here? I thought you and the robber baron had settled down for the duration. I mean, I thought I'd never see you again. I mean, it's okay with me. It's not your fault I am an extremely passionate and uncontrollably sensitive personality. I can tell you one thing. It's not easy being this sensitive. Oh, shit, he concluded. I'll just go on and get drunk. I'm a match for her when I'm drunk. Drunk, I'm a match for anyone, even Nora Jane. He opened the closet and reached in behind one of Buiji Dalton's hand-painted Egyptian funeral urns and took out a bottle of Red Aubruch his brother had sent from somewhere. He found a corkscrew and opened it. He passed the cork before his nose, then lifted the bottle and began to drink. "There ain't no little bottle," he was thinking. "Like that old bottle of mine."

At about the same time that Freddy Harwood was resorting to this time-honored method of acquiring courage, Lin Tan Sing was using a similar approach aboard the Starlight Express. He was drinking gin and trying not to stare at the yellow stockings which were all he could see of Nora Jane. She was in a high-backed swivel chair turned around to look out the glassed-in back of the train. She was thinking about whales, how they had their babies in the water, and also about Sandra Draine, who had a baby in a tub of saltwater in Sausalito while her husband videotaped the birth. They had shown the tape at the gallery when Sandra had her fall show. It won't be like that for me, Nora Jane was thinking. I'm not letting anyone take any pictures or even come in the room except the doctor and maybe Freddy, but no cameras. I know he'll want to bring a camera, if he's there. He's the silliest man I have ever known.

But I love him anyway. And I hate to do this to him but I have to do what I have to do. I can't be alone now. I have to go somewhere. The train rounded a curve. The wheels screeched. Nora Jane's chair swiveled around. Her feet flew out and she hit Lin Tan in the knee with a ballet shoe.

"Oh, my God," she said. "Did I hurt you?"

"It is nothing."

"We hit a curve. I'm really sorry. I thought the chair was fastened down."

"You are going to have a baby?" His face was very close to her face. It was the largest oriental face Nora Jane had ever seen. The darkest eyes. She had not known there were eyes that dark in all the world, even in China. She lowered her own.

"Yes," she said. "I am."

"I am geneticist. This interests me very much."

"It does me too."

"Would you like to talk with me?"

"Sure. I'd like to have someone to talk to. I was just thinking about the whales. I guess they don't even know it's cold, do they?"

"I have gone out in kayak to be near them. It is very mysterious. It was the best experience I have had in California. A friend of mine in lab at Berkeley Women's

Clinic took me with him. He heads a team of volunteers to collect money for whales. Next summer I will go again."

"Oh, my God. That's where I go. I mean, that's my doctor. I'm going to have twin baby girls. I had an amnio at your clinic. That's how I know what they are."

"Oh, this is very strange. You are Miss Whittington of 1512 Arch Street, is it not so? Oh, this is very strange meeting. I am head technician at this lab. Head technician for night lab. Yes. I am the one who did the test for you. I was very excited to have these twin girls show up. It was an important day for me. I had just been given great honor at the university. Oh, this is chance meeting like in books." He stood up and took her hand. "I am Lin Tan Sing, of the province of Suchow, near Beijing, in Central China. I am honored to make your acquaintance." He stood above her, waiting.

"I am Nora Jane Whittington, of New Orleans, Louisiana, and San Jose, California. And Berkeley. I am glad to meet you also. What all did the tests show? What did they look like under the microscope? Do you remember anything else about it?"

"Oh, it is not in lab that I learn things of substance. Only chip away at physical world in lab. Very humble. Because it was a memorable day in my own life I took great liberty and cast *I Ching* for your daughters. I saw great honors for them and gifts of music brought to the world."

"Oh, my God," Nora Jane said. She leaned toward him. "I can't believe I met you on this train." Snowy mountains, Lin Tan was thinking. Peony and butterfly. Redbird in the shade of willows.

Later a waiter came through the club car and Lin Tan

advised Nora Jane to have an egg salad sandwich and a carton of milk. "I am surprised they allow you to travel so far along in your pregnancy. Are you going far?"

"Oh, no one said I could go. I mean, I didn't ask anyone. They said I could travel until two months before they came." She put her hand to her mouth. "I guess I should have asked someone. But I was real upset about something and I needed to come up here. I need to see this friend of mine."

"Be sure and get plenty of rest tonight. Very heavy burden for small body."

"My body's not so small. I have big bones. See my wrists." She held out her wrists and he pretended to be amazed at their size. "All the same, be sure and rest tomorrow. Don't take chances. Many very small babies at clinic now. I am worrying very much about so many months in machine for tiny babies. Still, it is United States and they will not allow anything to die. It is the modern age."

"I want my babies no matter what size they are." She folded her hands across her lap. "I guess I shouldn't have come up here. Well, it's too late now. Anyway, where did you learn to speak English so well? Did you have it in school?"

"I studied your writers. I studied Ernest Hemingway and William Faulkner and John Dos Passos. Also, many American poets. Then, since I am here, I am learning all the time with my ears."

"I like poetry a lot. I'm crazy about it to tell the truth."

"I am going to translate poetry of women in my country for women of America. I have noticed there is much sadness and menustation in poetry of women here. But is not sadness in life here. In my country poetry is to overcome sadness, help people to understand how things are and see beauty and order and not give in to despair."

"Oh, like what? Tell me some."

"Here is poem by famous poet of the T'ang Dynasty. The golden age of Chinese poetry."

> *A branch is torn from the tree*
> *The tree does not grieve*
> *And goes on growing*

"Oh, that's wonderful."

"This poet is called the White Poppy. She has been dead for hundreds of years but her poems will always live. This is how it is with the making of beautiful things, don't you find it so?"

"Whenever I think of being on this train I'll remember you telling me that poem." She was embarrassed and lowered her eyes to be talking of such important things with a stranger.

"A poem is very light." Lin Tan laughed, to save the moment. "Not like babies. Easy to transport or carry." Nora Jane laughed with him. The train sped through the night. The whales gave birth in the water. The stars stayed on course. The waiter appeared with the tray and they began to eat their sandwiches.

Freddy was waiting on the platform when the train arrived at the Noyo—Point Cabrillo Station. He was wearing his old green stadium coat and carrying a blanket. Nora Jane stepped down from the train and kissed him on the cheek. Lin Tan pressed his face against the window and smiled and waved. Nora Jane waved back. "That's my new friend," she said. "He gave me his address in Berkeley. He's a scientist. Get this. He did the amnio on Lydia and Tammili. Can you believe it? Can anybody believe the stuff that happens?"

Freddy wrapped the blanket around her shoulders. "I thought you might like to see a movie before we go back. *The Night of the Shooting Stars* is playing at the Courthouse in Willets."

"He ran off and left me," she said. "I knew he would. I don't think I even care."

"You met the guy on the train that did the amnio? I don't believe it."

"He knew my name. I almost fainted when he said it."

"Look, we don't have to go to a movie unless you feel like it. I just noticed it was playing. It's got a pregnant woman in it."

"I've seen it three times. We went last year, don't you remember? But I'll go again if you want to."

"We could eat instead. Have you eaten anything?"

"I had a sandwich on the train. I guess we better go on to the house. I'm supposed to take it easy. I don't have any luggage. I just brought this duffel bag. I was too mad to pack."

"We'll get something to eat." He took her arm and pulled her close to him. Her skin beneath her sleeve was the same as the last time he had touched her. They began to move in the direction of the car. "I love the way you smell," she said. "You always smell just like you are. Listen, Freddy, I don't know exactly what I'm doing right now. I'm just doing the best I can and playing it by ear. But I'm okay. I really am okay. Do you believe everything that's happened?"

"You want to buy anything? Is there anything you need? You want to see a doctor or anything like that?"

"No, let's just go up to the house. I've been thinking about the house a lot. About the windows. Did you get the rest of them put in?"

"Yeah, and now the goddamn birds are going crazy crashing into them. Five dead birds this week. They fight their reflections. How's that for a metaphor." He helped her into the car. "Wear your seat belt, okay? So, what's going on inside there?"

"They just move around all the time. If I need to I can sell the car. I don't want anybody supporting us, even you. I'm really doing great. I don't know all the details yet but I'm figuring things out." He started the motor and began to drive. She reached over and touched his knee. They drove through the town of Fort Bragg and turned onto the road to Willets. Nora Jane moved her hand and fell asleep curled up on the seat. She didn't wake again until they were past Willets and had started up the long hill leading to the gravel road that led to the broken path to Freddy's house. "He said they were going to give great gifts to the world, gifts of music," she said, when she woke. "I think it means they won't be afraid to sing in public. I want to call Li Suyin and talk to her about it. I forgot you didn't have a phone. I need to call and tell her where I am. If she calls San Jose she'll start worrying about me."

"You can call tomorrow. Look, how about putting your hand back on my leg. That way I'll believe you're here." He looked at her. "I want to believe you're here."

"You're crazy to even talk to me."

"No, I'm not. I'm the sane one, remember, the control in the modern world experiment." She was laughing now so he could afford to look at her as hard as he liked. She looked okay. Tired and not much color in her face, but okay. Perfect as always from Freddy Harwood's point of view.

II

"I want to take them on the grand tour as soon as they're old enough," Freddy was saying. They were lying on a futon on top of a mattress in the smallest of the upstairs rooms. "My grandmother took me when I was twelve. She took my cousin, Sally, and hired a gigolo to dance with her in Vienna. I had this navy blue raincoat with a zip-in lining. God, I wish I still had that coat." Nora Jane snuggled down beside him, smelling his chest. It smelled like a wild animal. There were many things about Freddy Harwood that excited her almost as much as love. She patted him on the arm. "So, anyway," he continued. "I have this uncle in New Orleans and he's married two women with three children. He's raised six children that didn't belong to him and he's getting along all right. He says at least his subconscious isn't involved. There's a lot to be said for that. . . . What I'm saying is, I haven't lived in Berkeley all my life to give in to some kind of old worn-out masculine pride. Not with all the books I've read."

"All I've ever done is make you sad. I always end up doing something mean to you."

"Maybe I like it. Anyway, you're here and that's how it is. But we ought to go back to town in a few days. You can stay with me there, can't you?" He pulled her closer, as close as he dared. She was so soft. The babies only made her softer. "I ought to call Stuart and tell him you're here."

"He's a heart doctor. He doesn't know anything about babies."

"Wait a minute. One of them did something. Oh, shit, did you feel that?"

"I know. They're in there. Sometimes I forget it but not very often. Tell me some more about when you went to Europe. Tell me everything you can remember, just the way it happened. Like what you had to eat and what everyone was wearing."

"Okay. Sally had a navy blue skirt and a jacket and she had some white blouses and in Paris we got some scarves. She had this scarf with the Visigoth crowns on it and she had it tied in a loop so a whole crown showed. She fixed it all the time she wore it. She couldn't leave it alone. Then they went somewhere and got some dresses made out of velvet but they only wore them at night."

"What did you wear?" She had a vision of him alone in a hotel room putting on his clothes when he was twelve. "I bet you were a wonderful-looking boy. I bet you were the smartest boy in Europe."

"We met Jung. We talked to him. So, what else did you talk about to this Chinese research biologist?"

"A genetic research biologist. He's still studying it. He has to finish school before he can do his real work. He wants to do things to DNA and find out how much we remember. He thinks we remember everything that ever happened to anyone from the beginning of time because there wouldn't be any reason to forget it, and if you can make computer chips so small, then the brain is much larger than that. We talked all the way from Sausalito. His father was a painter. When his sister gets here they might move to Sweden. He believes in the global village."

"He says they're musicians, huh?"

"Well, it wasn't that simple. It was very complicated.

He had the biggest face of any oriental I've met. I just love him. I'm going to talk to him a lot more when we both get back to San Francisco." Her voice was getting softer, blurring the words.

"Go to sleep," Freddy said. "Don't talk anymore." He felt a baby move, then move again. They were moving quite a bit.

"I'm cold," she said. "Also, he said the birth process was the worst thing we ever go through in our life. He told me about this boy in England that's a genius, his parents are both doctors and they let him stay in the womb for eighteen months for an experiment and he can remember being born and tells about it. He said it was like someone tore a hole in the universe and jerked you out. Get closer, will you. God, I'm tired."

"We ought to go downstairs and sleep in front of the fire. I'm going to make a bed down there and come get you."

Freddy went downstairs and pulled a mattress up before the fireplace and built up the fire and brought two futons in and laid them on top of the mattress and added a stack of wool blankets and some pillows. When he had everything arranged, he went back upstairs and carried her down and tucked her in. Then he rubbed her back and told her stories about Vienna and wondered what time it was. I am an hour from town, he told himself, and Sam is twenty minutes away and probably drunk besides. It's at least three o'clock in the morning and the water's half-frozen in the cistern and I let her come up here because I was too goddamn selfish to think of a way to stop it. So, tomorrow we go to town.

"Freddy?"

"Yes."

"I had a dream a moment ago . . . a dream of a meadow. All full of light and this dark tree. I had to go around it."

"Go to sleep, honey. Please go to sleep."

When she fell asleep he got up and sat on the hearth. We are here as on a darkling plain, he thought. We forget who we are. Branching plants, at the mercy of water. But tough. Tough and violent, some of us anyway. Oh, shit, if anything happened to her I couldn't live. Well, I've got to get some air. This day is one too many.

He pulled on a long black cashmere coat that had belonged to his father and went outside and took a sack of dogfood out of the car and walked down into the hollow to feed the bobcat. He spread part of the food on the ground and left the open sack beside it. "I know you're in there," he said out loud. "Well, here's some food. Come and get it. Nora Jane's here. I guess you know that by now. Don't kill anything until she leaves." He listened. The only sound was the wind in the trees. It was very cold. The stars were very clear. There was a rustle, about forty yards away. Then nothing. "Good night then," Freddy said. "I guess this dog food was grown in Iowa. The global village. Well, why not." He started back up the hill, thinking the bobcat might jump on him at any moment. It took his mind off Nora Jane for almost thirty seconds.

At that moment the Starlight Express came to a stop in Seattle, Washington, and Lin Tan climbed down from the train and started off in search of adventure. Before the week was over he would fall in love with the daughter of a poet. His life would be shadowed for five years by the events of the next few hours but he didn't know that yet. He was in a wonderful mood. All his philosophical and mystical beliefs were coming together like ducks on a pond. To make him believe in his work, fate had put him on a train with a girl whose amnio he had done only a few months before. Twin baby girls with AB positive blood, the luckiest of all blood. Not many scientists have also great feeling for mystical properties of life, he decided, and see genetic structure when they gaze at stars. I am very lucky my father taught me to love beauty. Moss on Pond, Light on Water, Smoke Rising Beneath the Wheels of Locomotive. Yes, Lin Tan concluded, I am a fortunate man in a universe that really knows what it is doing.

Freddy let himself back into the house. He built up the fire, covered Nora Jane and lay down beside her to try to sleep. This is not paranoia, he told himself. I am hyper-aware, which is a different thing. If it weren't for people like me the race would have disappeared years ago. Who tends the lines at night? Who watches for the big cats with their night vision? Who stays outside the circle and guards the tribe?

He snuggled closer, smelling her hair. "What is divinity if it can come only in silent shadows and in dreams?" Barukh atah Adonai eloheinu, melekh ha-olam. Praised be thou, Lord our God, King of the Universe, who has brought forth bread from the earth. Nora Jane, me. Jesus Christ!

It was five-thirty when she woke him. "I'm wet," she said. "I think my water broke. I guess that's it. You'd better go and get someone."

"Oh, no, you didn't do this to me." He was bolt up-right, pulling on his boots. "You're joking. There isn't even a phone."

"Go use one somewhere. Freddy, this is serious. I'm in a lot of pain, I think. I can't tell. Please go on. Go right now."

"Nora Jane. This isn't happening to me." He was pulling on his boots.

"Go on. It'll be okay. This Chinese guy said they were going to be great so they can't die. But hurry up. How far is it to Sam's?"

"Twenty minutes. Oh, shit. Okay, I'm going. Don't do anything until I get back. If you have to go to the bath-room, do it right there." He leaned fiercely down over her. His hands were on her shoulders. "I'll be right back here. Don't move until I come." He ran from the house, jumped into his car, and began driving down the rocky drive. It was impossible to do more than five miles an hour over the rocks. The whole thing was impossible. The sun was lighting up the sky behind the mountains. The sky was silver. Brilliant clouds covered the western sky. Freddy came to the gate he shared with the other people on the mountain and drove right through it, leaving it torn off the post. He drove as fast as he dared down the rocky incline and turned onto gravel and saw the smoke coming from the chimney of Sam Lyons's house.

Nora Jane was in great pain. "I'm your mother," she was pleading. "Don't hurt me. I wouldn't hurt you. Please don't do it. Don't come now. Just wait awhile, go back to sleep. Oh, God. Oh, Jesus Christ. It's too cold. I'm freez-ing. I have to stop this. Pray for us sinners." The bed filled with water. She looked down. It wasn't water. It was blood. So much blood. What's going on? she thought. Why is this happening to me? I don't want it. Holy Mary, Mother of God, pray for us sinners now and at the hour of our death, Amen. Hail Mary, Mother of God, blessed art thou among women and blessed is the fruit of your womb, Jesus. Oh, Christ, Oh, shit, oh, god-damnit all to hell. I don't know what's so cold. I don't know what I'm going to do. Someone should be here. I want to see somebody.

The blood continued to pour out upon the bed.

Sam came to the door. "A woman's up there having babies," Freddy said. "Get on the phone and call an ambulance and the nearest helicopter service. Try Ukiah but call the hospital in Willets first. Do it now. Sam, a woman's in my house having babies. Please." Sam turned and ran back through the house to the phone. Freddy followed him. "I'm going back. Get everyone you can get. Then come and help me. Make sure they understand the way. Or wait here for them if they don't seem to understand. Be very specific about the way. Then come. No, wait here for them. Get Selby and tell him to come to my house. I'm leaving." He ran back out the door and got back into his car and turned it around and started driving. His hands burned into the wheel. He had never known anything in his life like this. Worse than the earthquake that ruined the store. He was alone with this. "No," he said out loud as he drove. "I couldn't love them enough to let them call me on the phone. No, I had to have this goddamn fucking house a million miles from nowhere. She'll die. I know it. I have known it from the first moment I set eyes on her. Every time I ever touched her I knew she would die and leave me. Now it's coming true." The car hit a boulder. The wheel was wrenched from his hand but he straightened it with another wrench and went on driving. The sky was lighter now. The clouds were blowing away. He parked the car a hundred yards from the house and got out and started running.

Lydia came out into the space between Nora Jane's legs. Nora Jane reached for the child and held her, struggling to remember what you did with the cord. Then Freddy was there and took the baby from her and bit the cord in two and tied it and wrapped the baby in his coat and handed it to her. Tammili's head moved down into the space where Lydia's had been. Nora Jane screamed a long scream that filled all the spaces of the house and then Nora Jane didn't care anymore. Tammili's body moved out into Freddy's hands and he wrapped her in a pillowcase and laid her beside her sister, picking up one and then the other, then turning to Nora Jane. Blood was everywhere and more was coming. There was nothing to do, and there was too much to do. There wasn't any way to hold them and help her too. "It's all right," she said. "Wipe them off. I don't want blood all over them. You can't do anything for me."

"I want you to drink something." He ran into the kitchen and pulled open the refrigerator door. He found a bottle of Coke and a bottle of red wine and held them in his hands trying to decide. He took the wine and went back to where she lay. "Drink this. I want you to drink this. You're bleeding, honey. You have to drink something. They'll be here in a minute. It won't be a minute from now."

She shook her head. "I'm going to die, Freddy. It's all right. It looks real good. You wouldn't believe how it looks. Get them some good-looking clothes . . . get them a red raincoat with a hood. And yellow. Get them a lot of yellow." He pulled her body into his. She felt as if she weighed a thousand pounds. Then nothing. Nothing, nothing, nothing. "Wake up," he screamed. "Wake up. Don't die on me. Don't you dare die on me." Still, there was nothing. He turned to the babies. He must take care of them. No, he must revive Nora Jane. He lay his head down beside hers. She was breathing. He picked up the bottle of wine and drank from it. He turned to the baby girls. He picked them up, one at a time, then one in each arm. Then he began to count. One, two, three, four, five, six, seven, eight. He laid Lydia down beside Nora Jane, and, holding Tammili, he began to throw logs on the fire. He went into the kitchen and lit the stove and put water on to boil. He dipped a kitchen towel in cold water, then threw that away and took a bottle of cooking oil and soaked a rag in it and carried Tammili back to the fire and began to wipe the blood and mucous from the child's hair. Then he put Tammili down and picked up Lydia and cleaned her for a while. They were both crying, very small yelps like no sound he had ever heard. Nora Jane lay on the floor covered with a red wool blanket soaked in blood and Freddy kept on counting. Seven hundred and seventeen. Seven hundred and eighteen. Seven hundred and nineteen. He found more towels and made a nest for the babies in the chair and knelt beside them, patting and stirring them with his hands until he heard the cars drive up and the helicopter blades descending to the cleared place beside the cistern. Barukh atah Adonai eloheinu, melekh ha-olam, he was saying. Praised be thou, Lord our God, King of the Universe, who has brought forth bread from the earth. Praised be thou, inventor of helicopters, miner of steel, king of applied science. Oh, shit, thank God, they're here.

When Nora Jane came to, the helicopter pilot was on top of her, Freddy was doing something with her arms, and people were moving around the room. A man in a leather jacket was holding the twins. "They're going to freeze," she said. "I want to see them. I think I died. I died, didn't I?" The pilot moved away. Freddy propped her body up with his own and Sam tucked a blanket around her legs. "The ambulance is coming," he said. "It's okay. Everyone's okay."

"I died and it was light, like walking through a field of light. A fog made out of light. Do you think it's really like that or only shock?"

"Oh, honey," Freddy crooned into her hair. "It was the end of light. Listen, they're so cute. Wait till you see them. They're like little kittens or mice, like baby mice. They have black hair. Listen, they imprinted on my black cashmere coat. God knows what will happen now."

"I want to see them if nobody minds too much," she said. The man in the leather jacket brought them to her. She tried to reach out for them but her arms were too tired to move. "You just be still," the pilot said. "I'm Doctor Windom from the Sausalito Air Emergency Service. We were in the neighborhood. I'm sorry it took so long. We had to make three passes to find the clearing. Well, a ground crew is coming up the hill. We'll take you out in a ground vehicle. Just hold on. Everything's okay."

"I'm holding on. Freddy?"

"Yes."

"Are we safe?"

"For now." He knelt beside her and buried his face in her shoulder. He began to tremble. "Don't do that," she whispered. "Not in front of people. It's okay."

Lydia began to cry. It was the first really loud cry either of the babies had uttered. Tammili was terrified by the sound and began to cry even louder than her sister. Help, help, help, she cried. This is me. Give me something. Do something, say something, make something happen. This is me, Tammili Louise Whittington, laying my first guilt trip on my people.

Light Can Be
Both Wave and Particle

LIN TAN SING was standing on the bridge overlooking Puget Sound, watching the sea gulls (white against the blue sky), caught in the high conflicting winds. He was trying to empty his mind, even of pleasant memories like his talk with Miss Whittington on the train.

Just Lin Tan, he was thinking. Just sunrise, just sea. Sometimes I go about in pity for myself, and all the while, a great wind is bearing me across the sky. He sighed. Lin Tan was very wise for his age. It was a burden he must bear and he was always thinking of ways to keep it from showing, so that other people would not seem small or slow-witted by comparison. All men have burdens, he decided. Only mine is greater burden. I am like great tanker making waves in harbor, about to swamp somebody. This is bad thinking for early morning. I am on vacation now, must enjoy myself. He sighed again. The sun was moving up above the smokestacks on the horizon. The first day of his vacation was ending and the second was about to begin.

A girl stepped out onto the bridge and stood very still

with her hands in the pockets of her raincoat. She was looking at him. Just beautiful girl, Lin Tan thought. Just karma. Twin fetuses inside Miss Whittington and now this girl comes like a goddess from the sea.

"Are you lost?" he said. "Have you lost your way?"

"No," she answered. "I just wanted to see the place where my cousin committed suicide. Isn't that morbid?"

"Curiosity is normal mode of being," he said. "I am Lin Tan Sing of San Francisco, California, and China. I am candidate for doctor of medicine at University of California in San Francisco. Third-year student. I am honored to make your acquaintance on lucky second day of my vacation."

"I'm Margaret McElvoy of Fayetteville, Arkansas. Look down there." She leaned far out over the rail. "My God, how could anybody jump into that."

"Water is not responsible for man's unhappiness."

"Well, I guess you're right about that. My father says religion is."

"What!"

"Oh, nothing. I didn't mean to say that." She straightened her shoulders, leaned down and looked again into the deep salty bay. Now the sun threw lines of brilliant dusty rose across the water. On a pillar of the middle span someone had written "Pussy" with a can of spray paint. Margaret giggled.

"Please continue," Lin Tan said. He thought she was thinking of the dark ridiculous shadows of religion.

"Oh, it's nothing. My father thinks he can find out what got us in all this trouble. He thinks we're in trouble." She turned and really looked at him, took him in. He was tall for an oriental, almost as tall as her brothers, and he was very handsome with strong shoulders and a wide strong face. His eyes were wise, dark and still, and Margaret completely forgot she wasn't supposed to talk to strangers. Something funny might be going on, she thought, like kismet or chemistry or magnetism or destiny and so forth.

"Great paradox of religion must be explored by man," Lin Tan said. "In its many guises it has brought us where we are today, I agree with your father. We must judge its worth and its excesses. I am Buddhist, of an obscure Mahayana sect. I am more scientist than Buddhist however."

"I'm nothing. My mother's Catholic and my father's a poet. Well, the sun's coming up and the gulls are feeding." Margaret pushed her bangs back with her hand. She smiled into Lin Tan's eyes. She wasn't doing anything on purpose. She was just standing there letting him fall in love with her.

"I am very hungry after night on supertrain called Starlight Express. It would be great honor for me if you would accompany me to breakfast. I am alone in Seattle on first morning of my vacation and need someone to ask about problem I have just encountered."

"Oh, what is that?"

"I am working part-time in women's clinic in Berkeley, near to campus to University of California. I am in charge of test results from amniocentesis, do you know what that is?"

"Sure."

"Some months ago I made analysis of amniotic fluid from one Miss Nora Jane Whittington of Berkeley. Was auspicious day in my life as I had been given honor by university for my work in fetal biology. So I remember date. Also, this test was unusual as it revealed twin female fetuses with AB positive blood, very special kind of blood, very rare. Often found in people whose ancestors came from British Isles, especially Scotland and Wales. So I wrote out the report and later I found I had made a mistake on it. I made a notation that the blood type is that of universal donor. I should have written universal recipient. Now, last night, in coincidence of first order, if you believe theory of random events and accidents, last night on the train I meet this Miss Whittington, now seven and a half months pregnant and in the course of our conversation she tells me how happy she is that her daughters will be able to give blood to whole world if needed. She has in her pocketbook a copy of the report, with this false notation signed with my name. I am not in habit of making even slightest mistake. Now I must decide whether to tell my superiors at the lab and spoil my record of unblemished work."

"Could anyone be hurt by this?"

"No."

"Then let it lay. Let sleeping dogs lie, that's what my mother says."

"Very wise, very profound saying."

"Well, I'm a teacher. I'm supposed to know things. I teach first grade." She pushed the hood back from her hair. A cascade of golden curls fell across the shoulders of her raincoat. Her eyes were beautiful, large and violet colored and clear. "I was on my way to school when I stopped by here."

"I will walk you there." His throat constricted. His voice was growing deeper. He heard it as if from a great distance. Just love, he was thinking. Just divine madness.

"Well, why not." She looked out across the water,

thinking of her cousin, dead as he could be. "I don't pick men up usually, but I'm a linguist. I can't miss a chance like this. I already speak French and Russian and Italian and some Greek. No Chinese, so far. What's your name?" She began walking down from the bridge. Lin Tan was beside her. The fog was lifting. The sun rising above the waters of Puget Sound. The dawn of a clear day.

"My name is Lin Tan Sing. Here, I give you my card." He pulled a card out of his pocket, a white card embossed in red. Down the center ran a curved red line. To remind him in case he should forget.

"I have to go to the launderette and get some clothes I left in the dryer," she said. "Then we'll go and get some breakfast."

Soon they were sitting in a small restaurant by the quay. They were at a table by a window. The window had old-fashioned panes and white lace curtains. A glass vase held wildflowers. A waiter appeared and took their orders.

"So this is the Tao on your card," she said. "I read a lot of Zen literature. And I try meditating but it always fails. My dad says the Western mind is no good for meditation. He writes books of philosophy. He's wonderful. I bet you'd love him if you met him."

"I would be honored to do so. I have wondered where the poets of United States were living. Where is he now? This father of yours?"

"In Arkansas. Do you have any idea where that is?"

"No. I am ashamed to say I do not understand geography of United States yet. I have been very busy since I arrived and have had no time to travel."

"It's a small state on the Mississippi River. We have wild forests and trees and chicken farms, the richest man in the world lives there, and we have minerals and coal. In the Delta we grow cotton and sometimes rice." She was enchanted by the foreignness of his manner. This is just my luck, she was thinking, to run into a Chinese doctor and get to find out all about China on my way to school.

"Oh, this is strange coincidence," he was saying. "In province where I come from, we are also growing cotton. Yes, I have heard of this Mississippi Delta cotton. Yours is very beautiful but no longer picked by hand, is it not true."

"Yours is?"

"Oh, yes. I have picked it myself when I was a small boy. The staple is torn by machine. The cloth will not be perfect. Perhaps I could invent a better cotton picking machine. I have often thought I should have been an inventor instead of a scientist but my mother died when I was thirteen so I have lived to save lives of others. I had meant it as an act of revenge against disease, now see it as finding harmony for life in its myriad forms. So you know the Tao?"

"I know of it. I don't know how to do it yet." The light of morning was shining on her face. Just face, he thought. Just light of sun. Just Tao. "It is the middle way, the way of balance and of harmony." He picked up a napkin, took a pen from his pocket and drew a diagonal line down the center of it. "This is the life we are living, now, at this moment, which is all we ever have. This is where we are. It is all that is and contains everybody." He looked at her. She was listening. She understood.

"I want to see you a lot," she said. "I want us to be friends." Her voice was as beautiful as the song of birds, more beautiful than temple bells. Her voice was light made manifest. Now Lin Tan's throat was thick with desire. He suffered it. There was nothing in the world as beautiful as her face, her voice, her hands, the smell of her dress. She took a small blue flower from the bouquet on the table and twisted it between her fingers. She looked at him. She returned his look. This was the moment men live for. This was philosophy and reason. Shiva, Beatrice, the dance of birth and death. If I enter into this moment, Lin Tan knew, I will be changed forever. If I refuse this moment then I will go about the world as an old man goes, with no hope, no songs to sing, no longing or desire, no miracles of sunlight. So I will allow this to happen to me. As if a man can refuse his destiny. As if the choice were mine. Let it come to me.

He closed his eyes for a second. Wait, his other mind insisted. Get up and leave. Get back on the train and ride back down the coast and enter the train station at San Francisco. Go to the lab. Work overtime on vacation. Catch up on all work of lab. Take money and increase holdings of gold coins in lockbox at Wells Fargo Bank of San Francisco, California. Spend vacation time at home. Go with friends to the beach, there is no destiny that holds me in this chair. Here is where I could prove free will, could test hypotheses. If not for all mankind, at least in my case.

"I would like very much if you would have dinner with me when you finish teaching for the day," he said. "I will be finding the greatest restaurant in all Seattle while you bestow gift of knowledge on young minds. I will tell you about my home and language and you will tell me of Romance languages and Arkansas."

"There's a Japanese movie at the Aristophanes. It's by Kurosawa. We could get a sandwich somewhere and go to the movie. I don't need to go to great restaurants." The waitress had appeared with their waffles and orange juice. "To think I started out this morning to go see where somebody committed suicide." She raised her orange juice. "This table reminds me of a painting I saw last year at the Metropolitan Museum of Art in New York City. It was by Manet. It was just incredible. I almost died. A painting of a bar with a barmaid. This sad-eyed blond barmaid standing behind a bar filled with glasses and bottles of colored liquid. The light was all over everything and her face was shining out from all that. It was real primal. My father loves paintings. We couldn't afford the real thing, but there were always wonderful prints and posters all over our house, even on the ceiling. This waffle is perfect. Go on and eat yours."

She took a bite of golden waffle soaked in syrup, then wiped her mouth daintily, with a napkin. A queen is inside of this girl, Lin Tan thought. She is a princess. He laughed with delight at everything she had said, at the light on the table, the syrup soaking into the waffle, the largess, bounty, divinity of the day.

"We will go and see what the barbaric Japanese have done with your film," he said. "Or anything that will seem nice to you."

"What time is it getting to be?" she answered. "I've got to hurry up. I'm going to be late to school."

They never made it to the movie. They walked for miles after dinner talking in all the languages they knew and telling their stories. She talked of the origins of language, how she wished to study man's speech and was teaching six-year-olds so she could investigate their minds as they learned to read and write. As they formed the letters and grew bold and turned the letters into words.

He told her of physics, of quantum mechanics and particle physics, the quark and chaos, a vision of reality as a swirling mass of energy bound into forms that are always changing. The greatest mystery is time, he insisted. Energy is held for a moment in form, then flung back into chaos, reformed, captured again, undone, done and undone, an endless dance which we glimpse when we hear music. "Man is the inventor of time," he said. "Only man has need of it."

"You don't care if it is meaningless?"

"Is even more beautiful that way. I think I am falling in love with you, Margaret."

"I was afraid you would say that." She stopped by a stone wall and allowed him to take her hands. "It excites me, the way you talk. But we have to be careful. I could just be getting you mixed up with my dad. He talks like that all the time. It's sort of made me older than a lot of people. It has made me older." She pulled her hands away. "I don't want to fall in love with someone just because he talks like my father. Even if you are Chinese. I mean, he is Scotch-Irish. His father was all Irish. We have a lot of Irish blood."

"The blood of poets."

"How did you know that?"

"Because I read your literature."

"Well, I'm not going to bed with you tonight."

"Oh, no." Lin Tan bowed his head. "I was not expecting you to. I will take you home now. In the morning I will come and propose marriage. But not until I know you better." He laughed a great hearty laugh, a laugh he had forgotten he possessed. It was the best laugh he had ever laughed in the United States. He leaned back against the wall and laughed for several minutes and Margaret McElvoy laughed with him.

"This is the strangest night I ever spent in my life," she said. "Come on, let's go home."

She took him to visit her school. On the fourth day of his vacation Lin Tan found himself lecturing on Chinese education to a combined first- and second-grade class. He told them everything he knew about grade school in rural China, then showed them a dance Chinese children learn to help them remember their multiplication tables. He had gone to Seattle's Chinatown and borrowed a traditional Chinese teacher's costume to wear to the school. Margaret sat in the back of the class and watched the muscles of his back as they moved his arm up and down on the blackboard. The soft blue cloth of his jacket rippled as his muscles moved his hand, and Lin Tan knew she was watching him and kept his body as graceful and supple as a dancer's as he taught. That night she went to bed with him.

"This might be too soon," he said, when she suggested it.

"It's too soon but I haven't done it with anybody in a year, so that makes up for it."

Then, in a rented room in a small hotel, with a lamp burning on the table and the sounds of Seattle outside the windows, they offered their bodies to each other, as children would, with giggles and embarrassment and seriousness, with shame and passion and a very large amount of silliness they searched each other out and made love, not very well at first, then better. "Here is where my knowledge of anatomy and obstetrics should come in handy," Lin Tan said. "Here is where the doctor comes in."

"I used to play doctor with my cousin, but we always got caught. We would put baby oil on each other because her mother was always having babies and we'd get it on the sheets, then they would catch us and take us off to the living room and tell us not to do it. You should have seen my mother's face when she'd be telling me not to. The smell of baby oil would be everywhere. She was a girl but we were only four so I don't think that means I'm a lesbian, do you?"

"What would you do with the baby oil?" They were lying side by side on the bed, talking without looking at each other.

"We would put it on and then stick this toy thermometer in each other. I guess that really was dangerous, wasn't it? Maybe that's what made them so mad." She sat up on one elbow and looked at him. "I wonder if it was made of glass. We could have killed each other sticking glass up our vaginas."

"Perhaps made of wood," Lin Tan said. "Many toys are made of wood."

"We could have gotten splinters. No wonder they got so mad, but I think they were really mad because we had found out about sex. They were so protective. They still are, to tell the truth."

"What would you say to one another when you would stick this thermometer into your hollow places? Did you say, 'I will diagnose you now'?"

"We said, 'This will make you feel better.'" She started giggling and Lin Tan laughed his great lost belly laugh again and they rolled back into each other's arms.

"Will you stay the night with me," he asked, "or shall I take you to your home?"

"I'll stay. When I do this I always do it right. My dad told us not to sleep with anybody unless we liked them enough to spend the night."

"And what else?"

"To call up the next day and talk about it. I mean, say something. Because it's pretty important, you know. It's not nothing, making love to another person."

"What did your mother say?"

"She said not to do it until you get married. She says it's for making babies, not some game."

"I would like to meet these parents of yours. I would like to talk with them."

"Well, if things keep going like this I guess you'll get to." She touched his hand. She was falling asleep. She left the waking universe and entered the world of sleep. Once we were always asleep, Lin Tan remembered. Slowly man has awakened. Oh, let the awakening proceed. Let us rouse to clarity and not blow up the world where Margaret sleeps. He stilled his mind then with a mantra of wind and water and slipped down into the ancient mystery of sleep himself.

In the morning they woke very early and talked for a while. Then Margaret dressed and Lin Tan walked her down to the car. "It is very awkward to leave someone after making love," he said. "It is very hard to know what to say."

"I know," she answered. "Well, say you'd like to see me again. That's the main thing anyone wants to hear."

"Oh, I want to see you many more times."

"Then come over tonight. Can you remember the way?"

"I will be there," Lin Tan answered. He helped her into the car and stood watching as she drove away. He shook his head. It amazed him that Americans worried about him finding his way from one place to another when the country was filled with maps and street signs. At the place where her car had been, several pigeons flew down from a roof and began to peck at the sidewalk. Lin took that for a sign and went back into the hotel and sat in meditation for an hour, remembering the shape of the universe and the breathtaking order of the species. He imagined the spirit of Margaret and the forms of her ancestors back a hundred generations. Then he imagined Margaret in the womb and spoke to her in a dream on the day she was conceived. Then he dressed and walked around the city of Seattle, Washington, all day long, bestowing blessings in his mind and being blessed.

As soon as Margaret got home from school that afternoon she sat down at her desk and wrote the first of what her family would later refer to as the Chinese Letters.

Dear Mom and Dad, Jane and Teddy and Len,
    I have met THE MAN. I'm not kidding you. This one is too much. I don't know where to begin. In the first place I met him on the exact place *on the bridge where Sherman jumped off. He was standing there when I got there. He is Chinese. Dad, don't go crazy. Listen to this. He is the smartest person I ever met in my life except for you. He*

*reminds me a lot of Professor Levine. I mean he has the
same kind of penetrating black eyes that just bore into you
and like you so much you feel like you have known him
always. He is twenty-five. He's a medical student (third
year) at the University of California at San Francisco
and has a job besides. He runs a diagnostic lab and he is
going to graduate with high high honors, then go back to
China to help his people. Please don't worry about this. I
had to tell you, but not if I get a lot of phone calls at seven
in the morning telling me what to do. Momma, thank you
for sending the sweater and the blouses. They will come in
handy with the laundry problems. Love and kisses. I love
you,*

> *Margaret*

She sat back, read over what she had written, drew a
few trees on the leftover paper on the bottom, addressed and stamped an envelope and stuck the letter
in. Then she left her apartment and went down to the
mailbox to mail the letter. While she was gone Lin Tan
tried to call four times. Each time he left a message on
her answering machine. The last time he left a poem.

> *Miracle of seven redbirds*
> *On snow-covered bamboo*
> *What brings them here on such a day?*
>
> *Miracle of a tall woman*
> *Watching beside me*
> *She bends her head my way.*

"By the poet Wang Wei from Qixion County in
Shaanxi. I am counting the moments until I am with
you again."

*　　*　　*

That night he stayed at her home. A small apartment overlooking the bay. A balcony was on the back. They sat with their feet on the railings and he told her about his work. "Then I will see into the heart of life, the very heart of the beginning of life, and, for my specialty, I am studying the beginning and formation of the human brain. At a moment soon after conception one cell of the zygote splits off and decides to become brain. After that moment, that cell and all its progeny become the brain stem and the brain, the miraculous brain of man. This happens, oh, a million times a minute. Everywhere on earth new people are being created. Inside women this miracle is going on and inside miracle, second miracle of brain formation is happening. Oh, problem is how to feed and care for them. There is so much work, it must be done. Must be done. It is very presumptuous to wish to do such important work but so my dreams are. Dreams often come true. If something is not within human grasp we can not conceive of it. Think of Thomas Edison with his dream of electricity. Light up the world. Yes, and my friend, Randal Yung of Pisgah, New Jersey, only this very week, has captured atoms in a prison of laser beams and is watching them grow. They are growing because he is watching. Is called the Bose-Einstein condensation and was only a theory until this week. I have been invited to go and view this experiment. Would you care to fly to New Jersey sometime to see miracle of captured atoms?"

"You know the guy in New Jersey who did that?" She had been taking a roasted chicken from the oven to baste it. Now she closed the oven door and walked over to the table where he was sitting. "You know that guy?"

"He is a friend of mine from boyhood. From village

next to mine. His Chinese name is difficult to pronounce in English so he has taken the name of Randal. We were sent to the advanced school together from our province. He is very advanced about everything, is very smart, is a great scientist. Randal wishes to live in the stars. He is a beautiful man. All the girls are ready to die for him."

"And we could go up there and really look at this?"

"Yes, we could."

"Then we have to go. My God, this is the chance of a lifetime. I can get a substitute to teach for me. I'll tell them where I'm going. Oh, God, my father will have a fit when he finds out. He adores physicists. He says they are doing things they don't even understand. My God." She threw her hair back from her face. A pot of green beans was boiling over on the stove. Lin Tan got up and took the pot holder from her and saved their dinner.

Later, they made love again. This time it was better than it was the first time since they were no longer afraid of each other.

It is a strange thing to make love to a member of another race. Exciting and strange, curious and amazing. The amazing thing is that nothing unusual happens. The foreign person doesn't turn into a demon or begin to speak in pagan incantations or turn out to be anatomically unsound. They just get in bed and make love with the same old set of moves and pleasures that have stood all the races in good stead for many centuries. This is me with this beautiful goddess, Lin Tan was saying to himself now, as he watched Margaret pulling a pink satin petticoat over her head. Just Lin Tan. Just Margaret. Just fantastic sexual activity of species.

Oh, if she will only love me I will solve riddle of cancer and also learn to operate on fetal heart.

"What are you thinking about?" she said. The petticoat was across her legs.

"I am thinking of the fetal heart. Sometime the valves develop in bad sequence. If the mother has been smoking or not eating properly or very nervous and worried. You must come sometime to my lab and see the sonograms. Very beautiful to watch babies like fish swimming." He was quiet. When he raised his head there were tears in his eyes. "Sometimes, by the time they are in our laboratories, they are not happy swimmers. Sometimes they are in trouble. Last week, we thought we had triplets on the screen. Much excitement. It was two little boys fighting to live. They had transfused each other through the common umbilical cord. So tragic. The mother was struggling and in pain. We delivered them by cesarean section and did all that was possible but they were gone by the time we got them to the incubator. Poor little mother. Thinking of this makes me wonder what has been happening with Miss Whittington." He got up. He was wearing a terry cloth robe that had belonged to one of Margaret's brothers. He walked over to where he had left his clothes and found his billfold and searched in it for the phone number Miss Whittington had given him on the train. "She should not have been traveling so late in her pregnancy. I should have left the train to see that she made it safely to a place of rest, but if I had done that I would not have been standing on bridge when you came out of fog bank. Like a goddess."

"You are crying over a stranger."

"All the world is one reality. Each man or woman is

exerting many influences every moment of day. This is the night I meant to show you my great zen lovemaking I read about today in a book while you were in school. Instead, I tell you this sad story." He stood by the bed-post holding his billfold, the drapes of the terry robe falling open across his chest and stomach. Margaret crawled across the bed and pulled him into her arms. She stretched him out on the bed and began to count his ribs. "I never had this much fun knowing anybody," she said. "I can't believe you left a poem on my phone."

"I must find a more romantic poem for you. I will translate modern Chinese poetry for you so you can know my country through its poets."

"You are going back there to live?"

"I am not certain yet." He closed his eyes. She will think me ignoble, he decided, if I tell her that I wish to stay in the United States and make money. She is daughter of poet, very romantic upbringing. "I wish to go heal my people," he added. "I wish to be noble physician so that Margaret McElroy will think I am a wonderful man and care for me."

"I do," she said. "What do you think I'm doing here?"

"Would you go with me to live in China?"

"I don't know," she answered. "I've never been there."

Her father called at seven the next morning. "What's going on?"

"Nothing's going on. I only met him a week ago."

"You mother's worried. Here, talk to her."

"Margaret."

"Yes."

"Don't do anything foolish."

"I'm not writing to you anymore if you call me up this early."

"Come home and bring this Chinese doctor with you. Your father wants to meet him."

"He's on his vacation. He doesn't want to come to Fayetteville, Arkansas." She looked across the bed at Lin Tan. He was nodding his head up and down. His mouth was saying, Yes, I will. Yes, I do. "He wants to," Margaret added. "He's here."

"In your apartment? At seven o'clock in the morning?"

"It's nineteen eighty-six, mother. Look, I'm hanging up. I'll call you later."

"We'll pay for the plane ticket. Get down here this weekend, Margaret Anne."

"Mother, I have company now. I'll call you later."

"Your father and I want you to come home this weekend. You can bring your friend with you. I don't know what you are doing out there, Margaret. If you don't come here, we are coming out there."

"I'll try. Wait a minute." She put her hand over the receiver and turned to Lin Tan. "You want to go visit them? Momma works for a travel agency. She'll send us some tickets. You want to go?"

"I would be honored to go meet your mother and father. But I can pay for my own airplane ticket."

"We'll come. Send me some tickets. Oh, okay. We'll do that. I'll call you tomorrow." She hung up and turned back to Lin Tan. "Well, here we go. Now you'll see the real me, I guess. My parents are wonderful but they boss us all around like crazy. You sure you want to do this?"

"Of course. It will be great honor and also allow me to see interior of United States. But I must pay for my own airplane fare."

"Don't worry about that. It's her perks, you know, she gets a certain number of tickets free. She gets mad if we won't use them. Well, I guess we're going then, aren't we? Imagine you meeting my dad. Just imagine." She moved closer to him and it was several hours before they finished their other plans.

Two thousand miles away Big Ted McElvoy was sitting at his desk trying to write a poem. He had been reading *The Seven Pillars of Zen*. The poem was subtly but not greatly influenced by that reading.

> *Hostages to fortune, what does that mean?*
> *A man should bow his head and watch his children*
> *Disappear? Has* given *hostages, a conscious act? . . .*

He studied the lines, tore the page from the tablet, laid it on a stack. He went back to the tablet, drew several parallelograms, then four isosceles triangles, then a cone. He got out a compass, measured the angles of the triangles, then laid the compass down and picked up the phone. He called a close friend who was a doctor and asked him to come by on his way home from work.

"I'm writing a poem about daughters. You might want to see it. Where's Drew?"

"She's still in Tulsa. She changed jobs. So what's up? I take it you heard from Margaret. How is she?"

"She's out in Seattle seeing some Chinese doctor she met on a bridge. It's too hard, Ken. It's too goddamn hard to do."

"She'll be okay."

"I don't know. I don't know about letting them go off to goddamn cities and start screwing anybody they meet on a bridge. Well, she's bringing him here Saturday. Jane sent them tickets."

"I'd like to meet this Chinese doctor."

"Damn right. That's why I'm calling. Come give me a printout. She says he plays chess. Come Saturday night."

"Sure, and Ted, I'll be over as soon as I finish up here."

"Good. Hurry up."

The beautiful and awesome scene when Margaret and Lin Tan arrived in Fayetteville, Arkansas. The progress of the car that carried them from the airport to the house where she was born. The embraces at the baggage claim, father and daughter, mother and daughter, mother and Lin Tan. They drove home through the campus of the University of Arkansas. The oaks and maples were golden and red and the Ozarks were a dark dusty blue on the horizon. The marching band was practicing in the Greek amphitheater. "Sweet Georgia Brown" filled the brisk fall air. Big Ted steered the old Buick slowly past the buildings that housed his life's work. Twenty-seven years of English students had floundered beneath the gaze and searing intelligence of Big Ted. But he was not teaching now. His face was straight ahead. His hands were on the wheel. His mind was concentrated on one thing and one thing only. To get to know this Chinese man before he pronounced judgment on him. He had been up since dawn reading the late poems of William Butler Yeats to fortify himself.

"Where were you raised?" he asked. "Tell me where you come from."

"My father owns small plot of land. He was doctor for our section for many years. Not member of party but looked on with favor by party. I am the oldest son. I was chosen to come here and learn Western medicine. There are many medicines and tools here that we need." Lin Tan paused. He folded his hands together. "I will graduate with highest honors. Perhaps at head of class. At least in number-two spot."

"How do you know Randal Yung?"

"Is cousin and boyhood friend from school. Same age as me."

"Have you talked to him since he did it?"

"Oh, yes. Several times."

"What did he see?"

"Atoms swimming in thick honey of light. Very confused activity. Random and unpredictable. Entropy setting in. Disequilibrium. Atoms are moving very slowly now. Like death of organism, he says."

"We'll talk when we get home." Big Ted shook his head, as if to say, Don't talk about this in front of the women. In the back seat Jane McElvoy gave her daughter a look and Margaret McElvoy returned the look.

They pulled into the driveway of the house. A frame house painted blue with white trim. An old-fashioned screened-in porch with two porch swings ran across the front of the house. Gardens with chrysanthemums blooming bordered the porch and the sidewalk leading from the driveway. A silver maple in full fall color commanded the yard. A sleepy old fox terrier guarded the stairs. "This is it," Margaret said. "This is where I live."

"Come on in," Big Ted said to Lin Tan. "We'll talk in my office."

They brought the suitcases inside and put them on the beds in the downstairs bedrooms, then the two men walked down a hall and out the back door to a small building beside a vegetable garden. "Office," it said on the door, and Big Ted formally and with graciousness escorted Lin Tan into his place of business. Held the door open for him, then waved him to the place of honor in a brown leather chair beside a desk. The office had been made from an old double garage. The walls of the room were lined with books, poems in glass frames, posters from museums. Propped against the books were other poems, framed and glued to pieces of cardboard or attached to the spines of books by paper clips. This is part of one of the poems Lin Tan could read from where he was sitting.

> *They flee from me that sometime did me seek*
> *With naked foot, stalking in my chamber.*
> *I have seen them gentle, tame and meek,*
> *That now are wild, and do not remember*
> *That sometime they put themselves in danger*
> *To take bread at my hand; and now they range,*
> *Busily seeking with a continual change,*
>
> > *Thanked be to fortune it hath been otherwise,*
> *Twenty times better; but once in special,*
> *In thin array, after a pleasant guise,*
> *When her loose gown from her shoulders did fall,*
> *And she me caught in her arms long and small,*
> *Therewithal sweetly did me kiss,*
> *And softly said, "Dear heart, how like you this?"* . . .

"So you are going back to China when you finish your degree?" Big Ted said.

"No, first I have to do my residency."

"Where will that be?"

"I am not certain yet. Perhaps on East Coast or in Seattle."

"If you're one or two you ought to have your choice."

"Perhaps. They have not written to me yet."

"Then what? After you finish your residency?"

"It will take several years. I wish to operate on fetal heart. Also, to pursue studies of child development."

"You've got that pretty well knocked in your culture. Why study it here?"

"I might remain in this country. Perhaps mental aspects of child rearing are key to all health, or perhaps all is genes, chromosome charts of children with lymphomas are very interesting. Perhaps we can teach body of child to heal itself. If mothers can be taught to carry babies in their arms for one year after birth. But this is all theory of mine."

"No, it's common sense. Difficult to teach in the United States in nineteen eighty-six." Big Ted sighed. He looked across the desk at the young man. The energy flowed from Lin Tan's body, made an aura around him. It was going to be okay. I did good, Big Ted thought. Goddammit, I raised a girl with a brain in her head, hitting on all cylinders the morning she plucked this one from the sea. So, we'll let go. Let her go. Lose her. Maybe never see her again. Goddammit, she could wind up in a rice field or a prison. No, not with this man. He could take care of her.

Big Ted sighed again. He reached into a drawer of

the desk and took out a bottle of whiskey and two small glasses. "You want a drink of whiskey?"

"You are worried about something? Tell me what you are thinking."

"I'm thinking you'll take my daughter to a communist country and I can't protect her there. Convince me I'm wrong."

"I might not return to my country. I have done a wrong thing. I have allowed her to think I am hero who would give up opportunity to stay in the United States and be a wealthy man to go back and serve my people. It was unworthy subterfuge." Lin Tan looked Big Ted straight in the eye. Outside someone was knocking on the door. "Lin Tan." It was Margaret's voice. "Come to the phone. It's a man at Johns Hopkins calling you. It's the dean of Johns Hopkins."

"There goes your noble subterfuge," Big Ted said. "Go and answer it."

They were offering Lin Tan the moon and he said yes, he would be glad to come and take it. Later that night he asked Margaret very formally to be his wife and she accepted and Big Ted and Jane got on the phone and started calling their friends.

"Do we still have to sleep in separate rooms now that we're engaged?" Margaret asked her mother, later, when the two of them were down in her mother's room. "I mean, is it all right if I go in Teddy's room and sleep with him?"

"Oh, my darling, please don't ask that. I'm not ready for that."

"We're going to be married, Mother. Think how strange it must be for him, being here in this country, with us. I mean, after all."

"If you want to sleep with him go on and marry him then. We could have a wedding. You could get married while you're here." Her mother sank back against the pillows of the bed. It was a huge four-poster bed made from cypress logged on her grandfather's land. It had been a wedding gift from her parents, a quarter of a century ago, in another place, another time. Margaret's mother had been the most beautiful girl in that world. She was beautiful still, serene and sure, elegant and kind. Margaret hugged the bedpost. She was always a child in this room. All her life she had come in and hugged this bedpost while she asked questions and made pleas and waited for answers. Never once in her life had she been treated unfairly or unkindly in this room. So she looked upon the world as a place that could be expected to be kind and to be fair.

"It's too late to get married tonight," she said. "May we sleep with each other if we're going to get married tomorrow?"

"I don't want to discuss this any further," her mother said. She picked up a magazine and pretended to read it. "We'll talk about it tomorrow."

Margaret went to her bedroom and bathed and put on her best nightgown and unbraided her hair and brushed it. She put perfume on her wrists and knees and behind her ears. She opened the door to her brother's old room which adjoined her own. She gathered all of her old fashion magazines from around the room and sat down crosslegged on the bed and began to read. It was ten-fifteen.

Outside in the office Lin Tan and Big Ted were talking context. "It's got to be seen in the scheme of things," Big Ted was saying. "Bateson's got a nice little book on it. Trying, for God's sake, to make them comprehend they are part of nature. Poor babies. They've lost that in our cities. Poor goddamn babies. Makes me want to cry." He filled a glass with ice from a cooler, added two small jiggers of whiskey, and signaled Lin Tan to hand his over for a refill.

There was a knock on the door. Big Ted got up, opened it, let his friend Kenneth Felder in. "This is Doctor Felder, Lin Tan. He's our heart man around here. His daddy did it before him. This is Lin Tan, Ken. He got the big fellowship at Johns Hopkins handed him today. You two have plenty to talk about." He took Ken Felder's coat, motioned him to a red leather chair beside the brown one.

"So how do you like it here?" Ken said. "Have you figured out where you are yet?"

"Oh, yes, we studied a map on the airplane flying here. Margaret is very good guide. This country is larger than can be imagined from maps. We flew over mountains of the west. Very beautiful country. Here in your home is very beautiful also."

"Your own country's doing good. My wife and I were there last summer. We were impressed with the schools. She's a teacher, like Ted here. She had Margaret. She had all these kids. Well, we're all glad to have you here."

"They want to get married," Big Ted said. "Margaret's down there with Jane making plans. And I don't mind." He raised his glass in Lin Tan's direction. "The global village. Jesus, imagine the kids. And tomorrow we're going up to New Jersey to look at his buddy's atoms before they condense any further. You want to go along? It's Saturday. Call and see if you can get a plane ticket."

"Oh, yes," Lin Tan said. "Please go with us. My friend, Randal, is very lonesome for someone he knows to come and share triumph with him. He has been surrounded by reporters for many days now. We would be honored if you would go along."

"I can't do that," Ken said. "Well, Johns Hopkins. That's fine, Lin Tan. Really fine. You must have worked hard."

"Very hard. Also, very lucky. There are many fine students in class with me." He glanced at his watch. He sipped his whiskey. He stretched out his legs from the brown chair until they met Doctor Felder's legs, sticking out from the red one. Just Chinese man being enveloped by the culture of the West, he decided. Just one more adventure on the road of life.

"I brought the portable chess board out," Big Ted said. "If you're ready, we can play."

First Harmonics

RANDAL YUNG was sick of his atoms. He was sick of talking about them to reporters and sick of answering the phone and sick of people beating on his door. He was sick of everyone in the lab being green with envy and sick of the nasty rumors that his lab assistant deserved credit for the work and sick of people asking him if he thought he would win the Nobel. I haven't done anything to deserve a Nobel Prize for physics, he kept saying, wondering if it was so.

But mostly he was sick of the atoms themselves. They were in there dying a slow fat condensation, well, go on and say it, death. He was the first man to ever capture and kill an atom in a laboratory and he was dreaming of it. What sleep he had been allowed to have since the *New York Times* broke the story had been haunted by dreams of the nasty dying atoms. Fatter and fatter they grew and more and more the whole lab smelled of death, the death of atoms, the death of peace and quiet, the death of work. I used to be a scientist, Randal thought. Now I am a photographer's model. Now every kind of unflattering photograph of me is cropping up in every news-paper in the country and I can not sleep for hearing the stupid things they write about me. The Atom-King. The Boy-Wonder. The Young Einstein. My God, another week and I'll believe it myself. I have to get out of here.

He stood up. It was dark in Randal's bedroom. He walked over to an Indian prayer rug someone had given him at graduate school. He fell down on his knees and began to make a list. One, get a pale yellow bedspread for the bed. Two, buy six pairs of cotton socks. Three, have my coat cleaned. Four, tell Janet not to let anyone else come to see the atoms. Five, get rid of the phone.

"And we are here as on a darkling plain," he told himself. "Swept with confused alarms of struggle and flight." They are the first atoms ever captured by a man. They might contain the brain cells of Confucius or the Buddha. They might contain the dust from a beautiful vase. I don't know where we collected them. I wish we didn't have them. I don't know why I wanted them. Forgive me for getting them. If I get out of this I won't capture anymore. Well, well, well, well, well.

Randal got up. He padded into the kitchen and took a loaf of bread down from a shelf and began to make cheese toast. There was a nice new roll of cheese. He took it from the refrigerator and held it in his hand. It was good to have cheese. Good to have bread. Good to have milk. He poured a glass, drank it slowly while the toast cooked. I won't think about atoms, he decided. Atoms are nothing. Electricity and magnetism and magic, yes. Atoms, no. Atoms are a game. I ought to be ashamed of myself for telling those reporters all that stuff.

I knew it was going to happen all week, he had told

one. I had this very excited feeling and I knew it would happen. We were so near. All we needed was to train the lasers in a smaller circle. All we needed was a little luck, and suddenly, there they were. Yes, it was so gratifying, so exciting. Oh, we drank champagne and patted each other on the back. Thirty-two, yes, no, it's old actually for what I do. Lots of great work has been done by younger men. I'm old in the field. It was luck, yes, partly luck. No, it wasn't luck. There isn't much luck. You just set a course and do the work and hope for the best. No, I'm taking some time off. An old friend is coming. He's bringing his girlfriend and her father and her family doctor. After that I'm going to close the lab. Yes, well, they won't last much longer. Sure, we'll capture some more. No, not capture. No, I never said that. Some reporter for *Time* magazine said that. Well, no, of course not. That's enough. You have enough, don't you? Surely that's enough. No. Good-bye. Thank you. Yes, yes, no, no, good-bye.

Randal finished the milk. He was trembling. He couldn't turn his brain off. He opened the toaster oven and took out the toast and inspected it. He ate a small piece of the melted cheese. Then lifted the four pieces of toast onto a plate and took the plate and sat down at the table.

Yellow is the key, he decided. I will think of yellow. He looked at his watch. It was four o'clock. There must be a way to sleep. He began seriously and methodically to eat the cheese toast. Seven, he thought. Haircut. I have to get a haircut so I won't look like a freaky scientist on the Bill Moyers show. I don't have to go on the show. I can make them tape it and if I don't like it, I can make them throw it away.

Eight. I must look at the mail. They might turn off the electricity if I forget to pay the bill. Now everyone knows my name. I must be careful.

He ate the last piece of toast and shuffled into his den and looked at the pile of mail on his desk. He picked among it for the bills, found the phone bill and the electric bill and the water bill, put them beside his checkbook, began to sort out the other mail. There was a letter from his parents. He stuck it into a pocket of his robe and got back in his bed and pulled the covers up around his chest and opened the letter. The letter was in Chinese but this is approximately what it said.

Dearest Oldest Son,

We miss you very much. It was good to have your letter and to hear you are having success with your experiments.

We are sad to tell you that two of your golden fishes have died. The one called Empress died and two days later we found the one called Lily floating in the same place in the pond. It has been cold weather here the last few weeks. Perhaps they died of the cold.

We are too old to travel to the United States. You are good to wish us to come there but we will stay in our house and wait until you come to us.

We send you the love of your family and friends.

> *Your mother and your father*

The stillness of ponds, Randal thought. Light on water. Stones reflecting the shadows of pear blossoms. Small boy in heaven of mother's garden. He closed his eyes, thinking of his childhood. His family had owned a house with a small stream that ran through the back yard. He had been allowed to dam it up and make a pond for carp. Men came from all around the village to sit by his pond and admire his black and gold and orange fish. Especially two specimens sent to him by the emperor of Japan in response to a letter asking information about a certain species. Larger and larger the fish had grown. Then Randal had left and gone to California. Now the fish were dead.

Randal folded the letter and put it into the envelope and laid it on the bedside table. Then he turned off the light. After a while he remembered he was wearing his glasses so he took them off and laid them on top of the letter. I will think of yellow, he decided. Yellow silk floating in the wind. Out of whole spectrum always yellow has appealed to me. Yes, I will tell them. I am thinking of yellow. You have heard of yellow, have you not? Yellow silk, yellow light.

Isotopes

The Man Who
Kicked Cancer's Ass

FIRST MY GODDAMN HAIR FELL OUT. I wasn't going to get any pussy looking like that. So I gave in and got a hairpiece. Royals got it for me. He's about my size so he went down and got one and brought it to the hospital and I wore it home.

All this time, from the day I found out to the day it spread all over town to the day my hair fell out on the third floor of the hospital. All that time the assholes were waiting to see what would happen next. My friends were pulling for me and the assholes couldn't wait for me to disappear. Cancer, my fucking ass. I'd better stop here and describe myself to you. I'm a goodlooking son-of-a-bitch. Six three with blue eyes and steel-white hair. I've got six kids by three wives and four yard-children and nobody's ever heard me complain. You're in the garden and if you're a fool enough not to know the garden when you see the garden then go shoot yourself. I'm a heavy-equipment salesman and I'm the best. Ask around. They know Nat McFarland in Jackson, Mississippi. I never broke a promise even if I made it when I was drunk. So, the gang down at Poet's is waiting to see what I'll do with cancer, this shit eating up my guts. I must have got it the month I tried to be a beer-drinker. It wasn't a week after I went back to red-eye that the pain began and after that I was spending half my time in a goddamn doctor's office and then this chemo-crap. Lying in a hospital bed with my hair fallen out and too weak to even lay a hand on a pussy if I could have quit throwing up long enough to find one. There was this little roadwhore named Sally in here that Royals knew but I couldn't even get up the interest to talk to her. I'm in this fucking roll-up bed and two miles away it's five-thirty and the gang is getting together at Poet's to start the good part of the day. Where's Nat? I guess they're saying. Oh, he's lying up in Saint Dominic's with his hair fallen out and his dick fallen off. You ought to go up there and visit him.

Not a chance. They're not coming up here to watch Nat throw up and fill the goddamn room with a bunch of fucking flowers. I had a No Visitors sign put on the door. I let my own kids in and Royals and maybe one little roadwhore, this girl named Sally I've got the hots for.

So every afternoon I can hear them thinking about me. I'd picture the bar and Bill and Dutton and Reta Anne all down at our end moaning over the coming death of old Nat McFarland, who could drink anybody under the table and outfuck anyone in the whole state of Mississippi. It drove me crazy thinking about it.

Here's what I decided to do. No matter how sick you are from chemo there's a certain little slot of time when you feel okay. The trick was to make it happen when I needed it to happen, which was five-thirty on weekday afternoons.

I lay in that goddamn hospital bed and made my plans. Charlie Trane keeps an apartment in the French Quarter Inn across the street from Poet's. I knew he wasn't using it for anything that month as he had just married some roadwhore from Meridian and she had him so pussy-whipped he wouldn't even have a drink with you. I called him up.

"Charlie, can I borrow your place up by Poet's? For a month or two while I get over this chemo shit?"

"Don't run the goddamn phone bill up. The last time I lent it to you it cost me seven hundred dollars."

"It's okay. Don't worry."

"I heard your goddamn hair fell out."

"It's growing back in."

"Well, pick up the key at my office."

"You're a good friend, Charlie."

"Don't die on us, you son-of-a-bitch."

I checked out of the hospital on a Monday afternoon. I still had to go in every day and have my blood checked out, but aside from that I was free. So Royals helped me move and I set up housekeeping in Charlie's apartment right across the street from Poet's. We got this girl in to give me massages and stocked up the refrigerator with a bunch of goddamn orange juice and Royals goes downtown and picks me up a couple of suits. Dutton Marks keeps my measurements at the store so I didn't have to go in to have them fitted. I told him, send out the best, Nat McFarland has decided to live.

* * *

About two o'clock on Thursday afternoon I started getting ready, sipping orange juice and having the girl give me a manicure and glue the wig on my head. Then Royals helped me dress and at exactly five-thirty Jackson time I swallowed five milligrams of truck-driver dex and tied on my shoes and walked across the street and into Poet's. I am wearing this white suit that cost six hundred dollars and a light blue tie and I wander down to my end of the bar and order a shot of red-eye.

"Jesus Christ, Nat," the bartender says. "What the shit, man, we thought you were dead."

"It was hard. It was rough going there for a while."

"So you're feeling great now, or what?" He handed over a shot of whiskey and I held it between my fingers.

"I'm doing okay. I can't complain." I drank the whiskey and circulated around, nodding at a couple of road-whores I used to service and generally being noticed. I let about thirty minutes go by.

"Holy shit," I said, "What the fuck time is it, anyway?"

"Quarter after six, fifteen after." This from one of the whores.

"I got to get somewhere. Got to see a man about a dog." I set the glass down on the bar and laid a ten-dollar bill beside it. "I can't stay. Got to be somewhere at six-thirty." I patted a whore on the fanny and let myself out and Royals was waiting by the door with his Lincoln and he took me on home and put me to bed.

I pulled it about six times in the next month. Sometimes with Royals and sometimes alone. Once or twice with the massage girl dolled up in a dress we bought her. I pulled it enough. Old Nat's licked cancer's ass. That's what they're saying at Poet's now. Did you hear about it? Yeah, he was in here the other day on his way to see some roadwhore. Yeah, looking great, man. Looking like a million dollars. That goddamn Nat. They don't make them like that anymore. He's licking cancer's ass. You wait, he'll probably be over here before the night's over. That goddamn Nat. That son-of-a-bitch. They threw the mold away when they made that one. Would somebody bring me a drink? Goddammit, what do you have to do to get a drink around this place?"

The Song of Songs

IT WAS CHRISTMAS MORNING. A bright clear day. Almost cool. The city of New Orleans lay in peace. Sleeeeep in heavenly peeeace. Sleep in heavenly peace. Strains of hymns from midnight mass echoed in the ears of the faithful. For unto us a child is born. Unto us a son is given. The smell of lilies and candles. Morning. Children were waking. Cats prowled the marble floors of the mansions of the Garden District and the lesser mansions of the Lower Garden District and the Victorian houses of the university section.

Barrett Clare had slept like a baby on two Valiums and a Seconal, safe in the high bedroom of the biggest whitest house on State Street. She had fought for that house. If it had been up to him, Charlie Clare would have settled for the old Phipps place, that tacky brick box.

She opened her eyes. The sun was slanting in the wooden shutters, casting bright demarcations over everything on the floor, her red wool dress, her De Liso Debs, her satin, hand-embroidered slip, her underpants, her bra. She had slept alone in the walnut bed. I have always been alone, she thought, and rose from the bed, shaking off the fuzzy feeling of the drugs, worrying that Charles was already awake, looking for her. Her baby, her one and only love, her boy. Damn, she thought, and shook her head again. The Seconal was too much. That was going too far. Still, it was better than not sleeping. It was better than dreams.

She picked up the slacks she had been wearing the day before and squeezed them in her hand. She had been wearing them when the tall blond boy came with his terrible message. That nightmare. Only it was true. He had come out of nowhere at eleven o'clock in the morning on Christmas Eve to tell her where her mother was. Her real mother, the one that had borne her into the world and given her away. She never touched me, Barrett had told Gustave over and over. No, I know she didn't. I would remember if she had. No one can remember that far back, he would say, and move around ever so gradually in his old brown chair. An enormous response from Gustave. She never touched me, Barrett would insist. I know. I would know. They got me from the home when I was five days old. I weighed eight pounds. I was a huge baby. I was alone when I was born and I have been alone ever since. She had me and then she never even looked at me. Gustave would move again in his chair. When she talked of *it* at least he listened. Well, he always listened. He was a wonderful doctor. A member of the Academy. He was the best. The very best. The best that money could buy.

Where was he now that she needed him? Where had he gone to? How dare he leave town at Christmas. Why couldn't they find him? They could find him if they really wanted to. She sat down on the bed and rang his answering service.

"You know you can find him. You must tell him it's an emergency. Tell him it's Barrett, Barrett Clare. You must reach him for me. All right, I'll be waiting. Yes, please try." She hung up. Who do they think they are? Those answering-service people.

Amanda McCamey is my mother. I'll call her on the phone. The thought was like an arrow. It flew across the room and disappeared. No, it's her place to call me. If she knows where I am. Your mother is named Amanda McCamey and she is up in Arkansas and she is going to have a baby any day now. That is what the blond boy said. I am going there now. I will tell her that I told you.

I'll go too, she had answered. I will go and talk to her. You can't go, he said. She is going to have a baby. She doesn't know you know. She doesn't know I'm here.

I want to tell someone, Barrett thought. I need to tell someone who my mother is. She is so beautiful. Didn't I touch her? That day at Loyola? When Brummette introduced us. I think I touched her. I think I shook her hand. She called me Shelley. She thought my name was Shelley. Why hasn't she called me if she knows who I am? Here is your mother, the blond boy said. And now I am taking her away.

A rush of fuzziness passed across her brain. She shook her head. She picked up Charlie's coat from the chair and started going through the pockets looking for a cigarette. He had come in from Vail at three or four. He had tried to get in bed with her. "It was a snowstorm, baby. They closed the airport. I couldn't help it."

"Get out of here, you bastard. Don't get near me."

"It's Christmas," he said.

"Go away, Charlie."

She went into the dressing room and washed her face and hands. She combed her hair. She looked deep into the mirror, searching her face for the face of her mother. It was there. Yes, anyone could see it. I could go on living, she thought. If it never would be Christmas. If I never had to hang that dead tree in the window. Well, Charles will be waking up. I must act normal. I must act like everything's okay. It's Christmas morning. She laughed at that. Suddenly her sadness and self-absorption seemed the silliest thing in all New Orleans.

She went downstairs and found Charles and Charlie in the breakfast room. Charlie still looked drunk. He was reading the paper. Charles had already started opening his presents. "Daddy slept with me," he said. "In my bed." He tore open a package containing a white shirt with his initials on the cuffs. He pulled it out of the package and took the pins out and tried it on. He was five years old, a sturdy wild little boy, excitable, hard to control.

The shirt was too big. The cuffs came down and hid his new Rolex watch. "It hides my watch," he said. "It doesn't fit. You have to take it back."

"You aren't supposed to be opening things yet," Charlie said. "I told you to wait for her. Is Lorraine coming, Barrett? Are we going to have breakfast?"

"She'll be here later. She has to cook for her family. I'll make breakfast. How was Vail?" He didn't answer. She rolled up the sleeves of her robe and set the table with red placemats and a set of Christmas china Charlie's sister had given them the year before. In a while she put a breakfast of bacon and eggs on the plates.

"Let's sit together now," she said. "Let's hold hands and say grace. Charles, do you want to say the prayer?" They were holding hands around the table. She could feel the thick wiry hair on Charlie's hand, tough reddish blond hair. Wire, she thought. Like his mind. A piece of wire. I'll put that in a poem.

At least there's Patsy, he was thinking. God love her soft little buns. God love her laughter.

"Lord make us thankful for these and all our many other blessings, for Christ's sake, amen. Ahh, men. That's what old maids say, isn't it, Daddy?"

"You all go on and eat," Barrett said. "I'm going upstairs for a while." She reached over and hugged the little boy. "I love you, Sweetie Pie," she said. "Don't you ever forget that." Charlie sighed and put butter on a biscuit. He took a bite and put the other half on Charles's plate. They were beautiful plates, white porcelain decorated with holly. "I love you too, Charlie," she said. "No matter what you do." She gave him a very small kiss on the cheek.

"Don't you want to see your presents?"

"Not yet," she said. She unrolled the sleeves of her robe and walked out of the kitchen past the painted porch swing. She was the only woman in town with a porch swing in her kitchen. She walked into the hall and up the stairs past the stained-glass window depicting Saint George slaying the dragon. She walked into Charlie's room and took a pistol with handmade wooden handles out of a gun case and walked over to the window looking out on the avenue. Now I will pull the trigger and blow my old blue and brown coiled-up brains all over the Pande Camaroon and some will spill on the Andrew Wyeth and, why not, some of them can move out onto the balcony and festoon the iron railings. You know, they will say, those old railings New Orleans is so famous for? Yes, it will make a good story around town. It will make everybody's day. They'll forget themselves in the story of my willfulness.

She put the gun in her mouth and sucked the barrel. It was a game she liked to play. It was the only power she knew she had. The phone was ringing, a lovely ring, soft, like bells. Barrett took it down from its hanger on the wall. "Is this Barrett Clare?" the voice said. The voice was tearing into her ears. "This is Amanda McCamey. I am your mother. If this is Mrs. Charles Clare. If you are an adopted child. I am your mother. Oh, forgive me, oh, my God, forgive me. I need you so terribly dreadfully much. Will you talk to me? Will you let me talk to you?"

"This is me," she said. "I knew you would call me up. I've been waiting all day."

"I've been waiting all my life," the voice said. "Forgive me for calling you instead of coming there. I should have come. But I can't come for several days, perhaps a week. Will you come to me? Will you come to where I am? Will you bring your little boy? Your father will be here. I will have him here. He's the one that found you. I'll send him for you. Oh, yes, that's what I'll do."

"No," Barrett said. "Don't do that. I'll come today. Tell me where to go. Tell me how to get there." There was a sound on the other end, like sobbing, or something else, something she had never heard. "Don't cry," she said to her mother. "I am going to come to where you are as fast as I can get there. And I'm bringing Charles, my little boy. I will stay a long long time . . . I might come and stay forever. I might not ever leave. Can you hear me? I know you. Do you know that? I know who you are."

"How is that? How do you know?"

"I mean we met. At Loyola. Don Brummette introduced us. I used to read everything you wrote. I guess I had a crush on you that year."

"What do you look like? How could I not have known? I can't remember. So many things have happened today. A friend of mine was in a terrible wreck, someone I love. And everything else. Are you really coming here? You will come to me? You will come here?"

"I'm coming as soon as I can pack a bag and leave. I look like you. Yes, I think I look like you. We will look in a mirror. The two of us. We will look at one another. Tell me where you are. How to get there. How to go."

"Here's Katie," Amanda said. "She's my friend. She'll tell you what to do." Then a woman named Katie got on the phone and told Barrett how to get to Fayetteville, Arkansas, from New Orleans, Louisiana. It was not that simple. "I'll be there this afternoon," Barrett said. "Tell my mother that I love her. Tell her I'll be there very soon." She put the phone back on the wall and picked the gun up off the dresser and walked across the room and put it back into the case and turned the key. Then she took the key and walked out on the balcony and threw it far out into the branches of a Japanese magnolia tree. Then she ran down the stairs to her husband and her child.

* * *

Charlie was sitting on the floor in a sea of wrapping paper drinking a brandy and playing with Charles. The great hanging tree for which the Clares were famous on State Street swayed softly above him. "Well," he said. "You're going to join us. How charming of you, Barrett."

"My mother just called me on the phone," she said. "My real mother. The one who had me. I'm going there today and taking Charles with me. Now get up please and help me. I want you to call and charter us a plane. She lives up in Arkansas. It's a long way and inaccessible. Do it right now, Charlie. This is not a joke. Something's happened to her. She needs me."

"Your mother?"

"Yes, my mother. Please get me a plane right now, Charlie. While I pack. Charles, you are going with me somewhere. We're going to see your grandmother. Your real grandmother. Someone you've never seen." The child did not move, but her husband, Charlie, got up. He came toward her, reaching out to her. "All right," he said. "That's wonderful. What else? What else can I do?"

"What will we wear?" Charles said. "What will we take to wear?"

"It doesn't matter what we wear," she said. "We're going to see my mother. My mother. I'm going to see my mother." She picked him up off the floor and hugged him fiercely and danced him around the room. I exist, she was singing inside her head. I am here. I am really here. Everything that happens from this day forward will be better. Whatever happens next will be better and better and better. My mother is waiting for me.

*   *   *

A woman named Katie met them at the airport and drove them to a house on top of a small mountain overlooking the university. "It was brave of you to come like this," Katie said. "What a brave thing to do."

"Where are we?" Charles said. "I don't know where we are."

Then they turned into a driveway and Barrett's mother was standing in the doorway of a small wooden house. A tall woman with hair that fell like a cascade almost to her waist. She walked out across the yard and took her daughter into her arms.

Life on the Earth

WHEN WILL WOKE UP he was lying on a stretcher beside a creek bed that ran along a fault below the wide stone steps people in Reed County, Arkansas, call the Devil's Palace. It was still dark and the sound of the water rose and fell with the voices of the men around him. Three or four men who kept covering him up and asking him if he could hear. Will guessed he was on a stretcher. It was some sort of device, like the wagon they had used to bring him down the mountain when he broke his leg skiing at Targhee, the year he and Jimbo Creel ran off and worked at the resort and smoked dope all year, so long ago, it seemed like a million years had passed since the truck had come terribly falling across the road, since the car had spun out across the sky and he had gripped the steering wheel and felt his head fall into the window. His head was still there. Maybe his head was all there was now. A head lying on a cot in the dark beside the creek and all these worried voices drowning out the sound of the water. Snow, it was snowing. It was the sound of snow and he, Will Lyons, had fallen from the highway in a car and his head was still alive.

"I wonder if he knows it's Christmas," a voice said. I know, he wanted to answer, and, Tell Amanda where I am, but no sound came and his lips wouldn't move and neither would his tongue. Only part of my head, he thought. Some tiny little part right in the middle might still be alive. He closed that part down, like turning off a radio in the middle of a song. "Your kiss, your kiss, is on my list, because your kiss is on my list of the best things in liiiife." Yes, that's what was playing. That's the song the truck was gunning for.

"I wish he would talk," a voice said. "Because I know he's breathing."

"Don't wake him up," another answered. "For God's sake don't wake him until the ambulance gets here."

"I'm awake," he said at last. "I'm right here. Call Amanda, please. Please call and tell her where I am." A face moved closer to Will's, a tough dark face that smelled of machine oil. Its owner smoothed Will's hair, asked questions in a soft dark voice until the sirens began in the distance. "Here they come," the voice told him. "Coming to carry you home. You the luckiest boy I ever did see. You see that cliff you went over. There's no telling how you lived."

"Am I alive?"

"Sure you are. You doing just fine. Blood stopped coming out your leg and all strapped up and doing fine. Rainey's working on you. He used to be in the signal corps. Rainey, come speak to the boy."

"I've seen worse in Vietnam," the voice called Rainey added. "I don't even think you've got a break. You must be made of rubber. See that cliff you came from. It's killed seventeen people in three years. Got a sign." There were two faces above him now. One dark black and one light black. Other people were behind them and the sirens were louder now. "Rubber," the dark black voice was saying. "Boy here made out of rubber."

Then other men came and they carried him up the hill and loaded him into an ambulance and someone was giving him shots. One shot, two shots, three shots, then Will slept again. He slept while the ambulance weaved its way down the mountain and into Fort Smith and pulled to a stop before the emergency exit of Fort Smith hospital. Will slept and in his sleep he dreamed. It was a high school basketball game and he was the high scorer. His mother and father were sitting by the coach. His brother, Andrew, was holding his towel. Fayetteville was playing Broken Arrow. It was sixty-five to sixty-four, Broken Arrow's lead. He had the ball. He was running down the court. He was shooting. He shot and the ball went through the hoop and the game was won. Where is Amanda? he was asking everyone. Where was she? She didn't see me shoot. You're too old to be here, Andrew said. You aren't even supposed to be in this gym.

"I had the baby." Her real voice was on the real phone. In the real world. It was Christmas morning. "You have a son, thanks for not dying on me."

"Oh, no," he said. "Oh, no, it can't be true."

"He's got red hair. I'll bring him down there as soon as I can come. And my daughter Barrett's coming from New Orleans. Are you sure you are all right?"

"I found her," he answered. "I told her to call you. I thought you'd kill me for it, but I did it anyway. I'm sick of all these secrets. Goddamn, my leg is killing me."

"Are you all right?"

"I will be."

"Will?"

"Yes."

"I'll be there as soon as I can come."

"Bring him." He was dropping the phone. The shots were taking over. "I'm dropping the phone. They've got me all doped up."

"Drop it. It's okay. I love you."

"Okay. I love you too." The phone fell to the floor. It slipped down across the side of the hospital bed and clattered against the hard linoleum floor. A nice sound. The snow was filling the window above the bed. It looks like I'm going to live, Will thought. Jesus Fucking H. Christ, she's got the baby. What's that going to mean? But I'm alive, a live man who's breathing and his legs aren't broken and his hands work, he can do what needs doing. These are great drugs, man. I can see it all so clearly.

Will fell into a deep hard sleep. His mind gave up processing so much complicated stuff and his blood speeded up the work of mending his body and collecting broken bits and pieces. Jesus Fucking H. Christ, the blood might have said if it could talk. What is all this shit. What a bloody fucking mess. This is going to take months to fix all this. Look at these bruises, look at these cuts, look at this tear in this shoulder. Look at these lungs coated with nicotine. Work, work, work, fight, fight, fight.

Sixty miles up the long treacherous stretch of Interstate 71 leading to Fayetteville, Arkansas, Amanda lay back against the pillows of her bed. She curled the sleeping baby into the hollow place between her breast and arm. She touched his face. She examined the amazing length and perfection of his feet. She smelled and kissed and adored his hair. Adoration, she was thinking. Noel, Noel, Noel.

Mexico

Traceleen Turns East

IT WAS LAST May when Miss Crystal gave up on her diet and exercise program. She had completely lost heart and stopped caring. She began wearing loose shirts and Mexican wedding dresses. Caved in to fat. I had never seen her that way. Miss Crystal is the kind that never believes the handwriting on the wall, that always says, No way, José.

Why? I was asking myself. Why would she give up after all these years of keeping herself in shape? Why give up now? Well, the answer wasn't hard to find. After all, even Miss Crystal is not prepared to trade her teeth for a smaller waist.

Here is how the problem developed. First it became harder and harder to lose weight. No matter what Miss Crystal did or how many nights she went to bed hungry or how many breakfasts she skipped, still, the pounds would creep back on. One spice cake for Mr. Manny's birthday. One roast beef on the first cold day. One loaf of Mrs. Diaz's salt-rising bread and there would go all her work.

*   *   *

Finally, Miss Crystal was frantic. She went down and spent two weeks at a health spa in Texas and came home thin as a rail. Then her teeth started falling out. She had gone too far in the diet craze. First two of her molars became very loose. She went down to her dentist and the dentist said, You have been grinding your teeth to powder while you were starving yourself to death down at that crazy spa. This is terrible. We are going to have to send you to an expert and have him operate on your gums and no telling what all. It is going to cost eleven thousand dollars to undo the damage you have done.

She came home from the dentist and went to work flossing her teeth. I will make my teeth stay in my head, she said to me. The force of the human brain has never been measured. Anything the brain wishes, it can make come true. Only you must concentrate your powers on the thing you want. I am not ready for surgery on my gums. I am not ready to lie down and let my mouth be cut open. I will not take drugs and have surgery when my own brain can do anything it wants to do if I can only reach its ultimate power.

I was in agreement with her. You are right, I said. It only happened because you were determined to get your waist back. You just settle down and let a few pounds climb back on you and everything will be just fine. Look at all the problems we have solved this year. Crystal Anne learned to roller skate so she won't be left out of birthday parties and King is off of coke and has been accepted in a college and is madly in love with that girl in North Carolina. You and Mr. Manny have settled your differences and made a happy home. You will also solve this problem of your teeth. I know you will. I am sure of it.

Oh, Traceleen, she said, and threw her arms around me. You are right. A few pounds won't matter all that much. She pulled me over to a gilded mirror above the sideboard in the dining room. It is a very harsh mirror in a harsh light but we looked straight into it. "The body ages," Miss Crystal said. "We must learn resignation or die worse fools than we were born."

So we made a sour cream devil's food cake with icing full of chocolate chips and sprinkled cut-up chocolate pieces on the top and cut a piece and ate it while we prepared fried chicken for the Saint James Auction and Picnic for the Benefit of the Home for the Incurables. Every year we fry ten chickens for them no matter how busy we are that day. By the time we finished the chickens and wrapped them in red and white checked cloths and put them into baskets and delivered them to the home Miss Crystal was in a better mood. She had decided to go on and let the dentist try to help her. One look at the old people sitting outside in their chairs with their jaws caved in was enough to make her decide to go with modern science. I have never seen it fail that charity always pays off. This is not the first time I have seen almost immediate results from a charitable act.

While we waited for November we decided to try yoga. Miss Crystal found this young woman named Ruthie Horowitz who agreed to come on Tuesday and Thursday mornings and teach us how to do it. It is the ancient art of India and the kind Miss Horowitz teaches is called Hatha yoga. These postures, as they are called, are like very slow exercises. They stretch out parts of your body you didn't know you had and call attention to the fact that you are made of flesh and blood. Most people walking around now never give that a thought. They have forgotten they are breathing and think the main thing they are here for is to drive cars and go to the mall. This yoga gets you back to thinking about what you are really made of.

At first I didn't want to do it with them but Miss Crystal insisted that I give it a try. She is always worrying about my blood pressure so the first thing I knew there I was pulling myself into postures and breathing into my chakras, which is what you call the different parts of the spiritual development. This is all from the Hindu religion. My pastor at my church said not to worry, it wouldn't hurt me to see some heathen practices and might give me something to tell my Sunday school class about.

I have had to be at my church quite a bit lately, as I am a youth counselor in my spare time. We are fighting the dope as hard as we can down here but it looks like a losing battle. When I go down to the Saint Thomas Street project to visit people I know, these very small children come up to the car trying to sell us things.

This yoga teacher turned out to be more interesting than I thought she would be. I began to look forward to her visits. Began to worry that she might not come. We would take the telephone off the hook and go into the living room and light some incense and put on some very quiet slow music and then we would lie down on these sticky green mats Miss Horowitz brought with her and begin to do these postures, breathing all the time as deeply as we could to remind ourselves that we are not alone in the world but are breathing in the whole world every time we inhale. Out go the old things we don't need anymore. In come the new things for us to think about. In and out, in and out, in and out. They might be able to use some of this in the project, I kept thinking. We could get Miss Horowitz to tell the young people some of her theories. Miss Horowitz thinks young girls should not have babies. She believes in the early works of a woman named Margaret Mead. Mrs. Mead said that people should have to take a test to have a baby. They would have to take a test and pass it and then take out a special license to become a parent. She said no babies should be born to young girls who don't know how to take care of themselves, much less a baby. Miss Crystal was all ears since she had King when she was only nineteen and doesn't think she has been a good enough mother for him because of that. Everything he does she blames it on herself for being so young when he was born.

So we are doing this yoga for the months of September, October, November, and December and it was wonderful for our bodies and our minds. Miss Crystal returned to a size ten and I got my blood pressure down to one hundred and twenty over ninety which is low for me. Also, we had many wonderful conversations with Miss Horowitz about her theories and where she thinks the world is going and how to do yoga even when you are in a crowd or walking around the house. I learned to do a headstand and Miss Crystal mastered the Heron pose, where you stand on one leg for fifteen minutes without moving. We also gave up sugar, since Miss Horowitz is so against it, and we found we did not need it with our minds at ease. The fall moved into winter. Breathe in, breathe out, breathe in, breathe out. Miss Crystal had her gum surgery and recovered without mishap using the yoga to help speed up her recovery. We were getting so good at the postures that Miss Horowitz said we might become samurai before too long. Samurai are people who have become warriors and know that you must struggle and suffer to live and don't mind it or complain.

There was one other thing Miss Horowitz taught us that is interesting enough to mention. She had this idea that she could be a medium for passing along power from the universe into mine and Miss Crystal's chakras. It was the only thing she did to us that I worried about. She said not everyone can do it and not everyone is able to take it in but that when the right two people get together the one that is the go-between can take this stuff out of the air and pass it through her chakras into the chakras of the one that is lying on the floor. I watched her do it to Miss Crystal and then to one of Miss Crystal's friends that is a poet. The one that is getting the stuff lies down on the sticky mat (that is the name for the green mats we do the postures on) and Miss Horowitz goes into a trance to get the power to protect herself from being drained and then she passes her hands above the chakras of the person on the floor and very powerful information goes from her hands into the other person's spiritual centers. If she does it exactly right it fills up the subject's chakras without taking anything from Miss Horowitz but in the hands of the wrong person it could make the person doing it quite sick.

Miss Crystal and her friend, Miss Buchanan, swore they had never felt better in their life than after Miss

Horowitz filled them up so finally I lay down on the floor and let her do mine too. I know it sounds crazy but I think something happened to me while I was lying there. I felt like I had grown an inch but my husband Mark says that only proves once again there is a fool born every minute.

Mark was leery of this yoga from the start but he was wrong to be. It turned out to be a good thing we took that yoga and learned about being samurai. Who would have thought we would need to know so soon? Who would have thought an armed robber would show up on Story Street with a kidnap victim in the trunk of his car? It was three minutes until two on a Tuesday afternoon in January. I had gone down to the Rug and Flooring Company that morning and rented a machine to clean the orientals. I was in the process of cleaning up the mess when he came in, which is why white cleaning powder was spread from one end of the house to the other by the time the police finally got there.

I was vacuuming up the mess. Miss Crystal was in her office with a secretary dictating letters about the March of Dimes Celebrity Chef Dinner. She is the chairman of that this year. Dr. Phillips and his wife are going to participate and a famous physicist from here is returning to make Gumbo File and several others you would have heard of. The doors were unlocked, of course. Miss Crystal was born in the country and so was I. Neither of us are in the habit of thinking we are always about to be hit in the head.

Our doors will be locked from now on. You can be sure of that. We do not want to go through what we went through last Tuesday again. Although it was nice to have a photograph of ourselves on the front page of the *Times-Picayune* and the story was good publicity for the Celebrity Dinner.

Still, if I live to be a hundred I will not forget what it felt like to be running the vacuum sweeper and hear a footstep and turn around and there is an armed robber with his gun pointed at me. "Who else is here?" he asked, but I did not answer. I remembered the course in self-defense I took at the police department and I began to scream. I screamed as loud as I could scream. I was also looking around for something to throw out the window, hoping someone on the street would see a window breaking and call for help.

The robber listened to me scream for just a second, then he ran across the white powdered dry cleaner and grabbed me by the arm and put the gun to my head. About that time Miss Crystal and her secretary, who is really Miss Bitsy Schlesinger, a tennis player, came running into the room and when they saw us they began to scream. Miss Bitsy had taken a course similar to mine at Tulane and knew what to do. They screamed at the top of their lungs. Then the robber pushed the gun deeper into my head and told them to shut up or he would kill me. He made us sit down on the dining-room chairs and tied us onto them and then he went to the garage and opened it and drove his car in and got his kidnap victim out of his trunk and brought her upstairs.

It was horrible to behold. She was a lady almost seventy-five years old, as sweet as she could be. She had been kidnapped at one o'clock from a shopping mall and she was being held for one million dollars in ransom money. "But what do you want with us?" Miss Crystal said to the armed robber. "We have done nothing. We can't help you. You can't kill us all, can you? Who are you? What is wrong with you? Let us convince you to set this woman free and go away. Take my car. It's yours. There are the keys in my pocketbook. Take the pocketbook. It's got credit cards and money and a bank card. You can draw money from my account. You can take out two hundred dollars if you want to. The number is five five five five. That's the secret number at any branch of the Hibernia Bank. There is one only two blocks from here."

"Shut up, lady," he said. "I don't want to hear any more out of you." Then all was very quiet for what seemed like several minutes. You could hear the refrigerator hum and the air-conditioning unit next door in Mrs. Diaz's yard. You could see the dust settling down through the light beams onto the table and I reminded myself how short a stay there is on the earth under the best of circumstances.

"I'll bet you're hungry," I said. "Why don't you let me make you a sandwich. You can't think straight when you are starving to death."

He waved the gun my way, then sank down into the easy chair where he was sitting.

"What's this white shit all over the place?" he asked. "What's this all about?"

"It's cleaner for the dry cleaning system we rented to clean the orientals," I said. "If you want to steal something you should take them. Miss Crystal's brother sent them here from Turkey. They are original oriental rugs from Istanbul."

"What time is it?" the armed robber asked. "Where's a clock around this house?"

"Right there in the kitchen," I answered. "You can see

through the door." We were sitting around the rosewood dining table. Myself and Miss Crystal and Miss Bitsy and Mrs. Allison Romaine, which was the name of the kidnapee, tied to the chairs with package wrapping twine. The armed robber was sitting in the door to the front hall on an easy chair he had dragged in from the living room after he tied us up. He was a big man, wearing a nice open-neck blue shirt and work pants. He was a little overweight so his face was not as handsome as it might have been but he was still a nice-looking man. I couldn't tell how life had bent and shaped him into a criminal. It did not seem to fit with his appearance. I read quite a bit and at one time I made a specialty of murder mysteries so I know how to search the face of criminals to see if there is a clue to their motivations.

"You certainly don't look like a criminal," I said at last. "Also, I can see no point in us sitting here all day. What is the point of this?"

"I'm waiting to make a phone call," he said. "I have to wait for her husband to get back to his office so I can sell her back." He took a pack of cigarettes out of his pocket and lit one. No one said a word but in a minute Miss Crystal gave a little cough. I had never seen her that quiet for that long. I supposed she was terrified he'd still be here when King and Crystal Anne came home. This gun he had in his hand was a very terrible-looking weapon but somehow it seemed to me he would never really shoot it. Even when he had it pointed at my head I did not think he would pull the trigger. I guess I was having a denial. That's what Miss Horowitz said later when she heard the story. She said Miss Crystal was being samurai and I was having a denial. But later I also became a samurai when I had the brainstorm to fake a heart attack. She said the reason we were saved is that Miss Crystal and I are so used to working together and have honed the skills of cooperation so well that we knew how to read each other's minds when we had to. She said it is very interesting to understand the diametrics of a situation like that. She said what it looks like on the surface is very often not what is really going on. What it looked like that Tuesday was that everyone was scared to death. Miss Bitsy was breathing in little gulps, in, in, in, out, out, out. (She had not been doing any yoga.) Mrs. Romaine, the kidnapee, had begun to cry.

"Why me?" she kept asking. "Why did you pick out me?"

"Because your husband stole my racehorse," he said. "Because your husband owns the track and he owes me for ten years of my life if he wants to see you again. A hundred thousand dollars a year."

"I didn't do it," she said. "I didn't take anything from you." At that she began to cry louder than ever. Sobbing until I thought she might choke. She was tied up hand and foot onto a chair with a handmade petit-point seat cover of the coat of arms of the Manning family. She was too old to be tied up like that. I decided no matter how nice looking he was this robber must be the meanest man alive, perhaps a psychopath.

"Let me get her something to eat," I suggested. "She might get sick and have a heart attack. You might have a murder on your hands."

"Okay," he said. "Get some food ready. Make some sandwiches." He untied my feet and hands and I went into the kitchen and made five lovely little sliced turkey sandwiches with lettuce and tomato and mayonnaise and added some potato chips and brought it back on a tray. I set a place at the table for Mrs. Romaine and turned her around and untied her hands. So she could eat. I was thinking of things to poison him with. I thought of ways to grab the phone and dial nine for emergencies. I thought of how long until King would be coming home and how Crystal Anne would be waiting at her school with no one to pick her up. I thought of the time the bookcases in the den fell on me and Miss Crystal held them off with superhuman strength while I escaped. It might be possible to make them fall on him if we could get him in there. I thought of every weapon within my reach as I made another round of sandwiches. I thought of the dogs in the back yard. Three English sheepdogs that weighed more than a hundred pounds apiece. They were right out there in the back yard. How to get them in?

"Come on back in here," he said. "Stop fooling around." So I brought in the second tray of sandwiches and the iced tea and passed them around and then got back into my chair.

It was a quarter to three. The robber got up and made a phone call from the kitchen phone. Then he came back in. "I think I'll take that pocketbook you offered," he said. "Where did you say it was?" I looked at Miss Crystal. She was so quiet. She was breathing in and out, in and out, in and out.

"It's in my bedroom on the dresser," she answered. "Look, could I go to the bathroom? I need to urinate. Also, my children will be coming home. If you let me make a call I can keep them from coming here. I don't know how long you plan to stay, but surely you don't want my children coming over with their friends. You can't hold a dozen people at gunpoint, can you? What is wrong with you anyway? Why don't you let us help you? You don't look like you're insane."

"All right," he said. "You can go to the bathroom. I'll go with you and we'll get that purse. I'll need your car." He tied me back to a chair and undid Miss Crystal.

He and Miss Crystal went back toward the bedroom. Miss Bitsy and Mrs. Romaine and I were still tied to dining room chairs. Miss Bitsy was where he had put her to begin with, beside the sideboard. Mrs. Romaine was facing the dining table. Her feet were tied but her hands were free. He had forgotten to tie her hands back together. I was beside the rubber plant near the French doors that open onto Story Street. Behind the doors is a small balcony with a row of red geranium plants. It was almost three o'clock. Children would be coming home from school. If I could break through the French doors I could get the attention of schoolchildren and call for help. Of course the sidewalk is quite a way from the house. I didn't know what to do. I was thinking as hard as I could. Here is how a samurai decides what to do. One, he sees the situation as a whole. Two, he gauges his own strength. Three, he figures out the strength of his enemy. Then he fits it all together in his mind like a puzzle and finds the part that no one else can see. He must find the place where his strength fits into a hole in his enemy. Cutting my arms to pieces on the French doors did not seem to be a good enough plan. I thought harder. Who was this armed robber? What was he afraid of?

Miss Crystal came back in, carrying her pocketbook. She looked at me. I looked right back. I sent stuff to her chakras and she sent stuff to mine. "My heart," I screamed. "Oh, no, not my heart again." I pulled my chair forward with the weight of my body. I fell upon the floor taking my chair with me. "My pills," I gasped. "Miss Crystal, get my pills."

Mrs. Allison Romaine thought it was for real. She let out a scream. Then she picked up her sandwich plate and threw it at the robber. Miss Bitsy screamed too. "Heart attack," she screamed. "Call an ambulance. Get the pills for her. Untie me. I know CPR."

"Pills," I gasped. "Got to have my pills."

"I'll get them, Traceleen," Miss Crystal yelled. She ran from the room. The armed robber fell on his knees beside my chair to look at me. Just then the front door opened and King came in with his friend, Matthew Levine, beside him.

The dogs came bounding up the stairs. Tiger and Stoner and Boots. They ran into the room and started licking everyone in sight. Old English sheepdogs are the worst-smelling dogs you can ever imagine having. They are the last dogs in the world you want to let into your house and so kind they would never hurt a flea but the robber did not know that. I guess his guilt was so bad over kidnapping a woman old enough to be his grandmother that he thought the dogs had been sent from hell. He was screaming now. The harder he screamed the more the dogs licked and jumped on him. They sensed his fear and stopped being gentle.

Meanwhile, as soon as she opened the basement door for the dogs, Miss Crystal had climbed the fence and run into Mrs. Diaz's house to use the phone and call the police. They were not the first law enforcement to reach the scene, however. Our neighborhood guard came tearing in and disarmed the robber before the police drove up in three cars with their sirens running.

Mrs. Romaine was returned to her husband, who is a nice man who has never cheated anyone and ended up giving fifteen thousand dollars to the Celebrity Chef March of Dimes Fund. It put Celebrity Chef over the top and made them the most profitable charity event of the year. Miss Bitsy has been interviewed by three different publications concerning her role in the affair, including the *Tulane Alumni Newsletter*. They used a full-length photo of her wearing a white and green knit tennis outfit with a matching sweater. We are hoping it will help her catch a husband. She is so good at tennis it scares men off.

Miss Crystal and I have gone back to yoga. We are doing it for two hours every Tuesday and Thursday morning. No matter how busy we get we are in the living room with the phone off the hook two mornings a week doing our yoga postures. Both of us have many people depending on us. We must be strong enough to face the challenges. The strength to live your life and help other people begins in your own body. You must strive to make your body a strong thing that never forgets its place in the universe. Breathe in, breathe out. This is what Miss Horowitz is teaching us as we do the Plough and the headstand. We must be ready, she keeps saying. If is every person's duty to be prepared. Breathe in, breathe out. Just because we have faced one challenge doesn't mean there won't be another.

Mexico

JULY THE TWENTY-SECOND, nineteen hundred and eighty-eight, Agualeguas, Mexico, on the road to Elbaro, a Las Terras de Los Gatos Grandes.

It was the last day of the trip to Mexico. Another six hours and Rhoda would have been safely back in the United States of America where she belonged. Instead she was on the ground with a broken ankle. She was lying down on the hard stubble-covered pasture and all she could see from where she lay was sky and yellow grass and the terrible tall cages. The cats did not move in the cages. The Bengal tigers did not move and the lionesses did not move and the black leopard did not move. My ankle is torn to pieces, Rhoda thought. Nothing ever hurt this much in all my life. This is real pain, the worst of all pains, my God. It's karma from the bullfight, karma from the cats, lion karma, oh, God, it's worse than wasp stings, worse than the fucking dentist, worse than anything. I'm going to die. I wish I'd die.

Then Saint John was there, leaning over her with his civilized laconic face. He examined her ankle, turned it gently back into alignment, wrapped it in a strip of torn cloth. A long time seemed to go by. Rhoda began to moan. The Bengal tigers stirred in their cage. Their heads turned like huge sunflowers to look at her. They waited.

Dudley stood beside the fence. The lion was sideways. He was as big as a Harley-Davidson, as wide as a Queen Anne's chair. Dudley kept on standing beside the flimsy fence. No, Dudley was walking toward her. He was walking, not standing still. My sight is going, Rhoda decided. I have been blinded by the pain.

"Now I'll never get back across the border," she moaned. She pulled on Saint John's arm.

"Yes, you will," he said. "You're a United States citizen. All you need is your driver's license."

He carried her to the porch of the stone house. The caretaker's children put down the baby jaguar and went inside and made tea and found a roll of adhesive tape. Saint John taped up Rhoda's ankle while the children watched. They peered from around the canvas yard chairs, their beautiful dark-eyed faces very solemn, the baby jaguar hanging from the oldest boy's arm. The youngest girl brought out the lukewarm tea and a plate of crackers which she passed around. Saint John took a bottle of Demerol capsules out of his bag and gave one to Rhoda to swallow with her tea. She swallowed the capsule, then took a proffered cracker and bit into it. "Yo soy injured," she said to the child. "Muy triste, no es verdad?"

"Triste," the oldest boy agreed and shifted the jaguar to his left arm so he could eat with his right.

* * *

Then Dudley brought the station wagon around and Rhoda was laid out in the back seat on a pillow that she was sure contained both hookworm larvae and hepatitis virus. She pulled the towel out from under the ice chest and covered the pillow with the towel, then settled down for the ride back through the fields of maize.

"Well, Shorty, you got your adventure," Dudley said. "Old Waylon didn't raise a whisker when you started screaming. What a lion."

"I want another one of those pills, Saint John," she said. "I think I need another one."

"In a while," he said. "Wait a few minutes, honey."

"I'll never get back across the border. If I don't get back across the border, Dudley, it's your fault and you can pay the lawyer."

"You'll get across," Saint John said. "You're a United States citizen. All you need is your driver's license."

It is nineteen eighty-eight in the lives of our heroes, of our heroine. Twelve years until the end of the second millennium, A.D. There have been many changes in the world and many changes in the lives of Rhoda and Dudley and Saint John since the days when they fought over the broad jump pit in the pasture beside the house on Esperanza. The river they called the bayou was still a clean navigable waterway back then, there was no television, no civil rights, no atomic or nuclear bomb, no polio vaccine. Still, nothing has really changed. Saint John still loves pussy and has become a gynecologist. Dudley still likes to kill things, kill or be killed, that's his motto. Rhoda still likes men and will do anything to get to run around with them, even be uncomfortable or in danger.

Details: Dudley Manning runs a gun factory in San Antonio, Texas, and is overseeing the construction of Phelan Manning's wildlife museum. Saint John practices medicine on Prytania Street in New Orleans, Louisiana. His second wife has just left him for another man to pay him back for his legendary infidelities. She has moved to Boston, Massachusetts, and is fucking an old hunting buddy of his. She was a waitress in Baton Rouge when Saint John aborted her and fell in love. A bartender's daughter, a first-class, world-class, hardball player. Saint John has met his match. He is licking those wounds and not in top shape in nineteen eighty-eight. Rhoda Manning is in worse shape. She is fifty-three years old and she has run out of men. That's how the trip to Mexico began. It began because Rhoda was bored. Some people think death is the enemy of man. Rhoda believes the problem is boredom, outliving your gonads, not to mention your hopes, your dreams, your plans.

Here is how the trip to Mexico began. It was two in the afternoon on a day in June. Rhoda was in her house on a mountain overlooking a sleepy little university town. There was a drought and a heat wave and everyone she knew had gone somewhere else for the summer. There was nothing to do and no one to go riding around with or fuck or even talk to on the phone. Stuck in the very heart of summer with no husband and no boyfriend and nothing to do. Fifty-three years old and bored to death.

She decided to make up with Dudley and Saint John. She decided to write to them and tell them she was bored. Who knows, they might be bored too. Dudley was fifty-six and Saint John was fifty-eight. They might be bored to death. They might be running out of things to do.

Dear Dudley (the first letter began),
I am bored to death. How about you? Why did I go and get rid of all those nice husbands? Why did I use up all those nice boyfriends? Why am I so selfish and wasteful and vain? Yesterday I found out the IRS is going to make me pay twenty-four thousand dollars' worth of extra income tax. My accountant's computer lost part of my income and figured my tax wrong. So now I am bored and broke. *How did this happen to me? I think I have been too good and too sober for too long. Let's get together and get drunk and have some fun. I miss you. Where is Saint John? I bet he's as bored as I am. I bet he would like to get drunk with us. I heard that beastly woman he married was up in Boston fucking one of his safari club buddies. Is that true? I'm sorry I've been so mean to everyone for so long. It was good to see you at Anna's funeral. You looked great. Considering everything, we are lucky to be alive. Write to me or call me. Your broke and lonely and undeserving sister, Rhoda Katherine.*

Dear Saint John (the second letter began),
Let's get Dudley and go off somewhere and get drunk. I'm tired of being good. How about you? Love, Rhoda.

In five days Rhoda heard back from Dudley. "Hello, sister," the message said on the answering machine. "It's your brother. You want to go to Mexico? Come on down to San Antonio and we'll go to Mexico."

Rhoda stood by the answering machine. She was wearing tennis clothes. Outside the windows of her comfortable house the clean comfortable little town con-

tinued its easygoing boring life. Why did I start this with
Dudley? Rhoda thought. I don't want to go to Mexico
with him. Why did I even write to him? My analyst will
have a fit. He'll say it's my fascination with aggression
and power. Well, it's all I know how to do. I wrote to
Dudley because he looked so great at Anna's funeral, so
powerful and strong, immortal. The immortal Eagle
Scout who lived through polio and scarlet fever and
shot a lion, ten lions, a thousand lions.

Now Saint John will call me too. I shouldn't do this. I
have outgrown them. I have better things to do than go
down to Mexico with Saint John and Dudley. What else
do I have to do? Name one thing. Water the fucking
lawn? I can get out the sprinklers and waste water by
watering the lawn.

Rhoda slipped on her sandals and walked out the door
of her house into the sweltering midmorning heat. She
set up the sprinklers on the front lawn and turned them
on. Then reached down and began to scratch her chig-
ger bites. Fucking Ozarks, she decided. Why in the
name of God did I come up here to live in this deserted
barren cultural waste? What in the name of God possessed me to think I wanted to live in this little wornout
university town with no one to flirt with and nowhere to
eat lunch?

She pulled the last sprinkler out from under the
woodpile and set it on the stone wall of the patio.
Scientific method, she was thinking. Germ theory. I'll go
down there with them and the next thing I know I'll
have amoebic dysentery for five years. Saint John will
bring his convertible and I'll get skin cancer and ruin
the color of my hair and then Dudley will get me to eat

some weird Mexican food and I'll die or spend the rest of my life in the hospital.

Rhoda stared off into the branches of the pear tree. She was afraid that by watering the lawn she might make the roots of the trees come up to the surface. World full of danger, she decided. How did I come to believe that?

She reached down to pick up the sprinkler. Her index finger closed down upon a fat yellow and orange wasp who stuck his proboscis into her sweat glands and emitted his sweet thin poison. "Oh, my God," Rhoda screamed. "Now I have been bit by a wasp."

An hour later she lay on the sofa in the air conditioning with a pot of coffee on the table beside her. Hot coffee in a beautiful blue and white Thermos and two cups in case anyone should come by and a small plate holding five Danish cookies and an ironed linen napkin. She was wearing a silk robe and a pair of white satin house shoes. Her head was resting on a blue satin pillow her mother had sent for her birthday. Her swollen finger was curled upon her stomach. She dialed Dudley's number and the phone in San Antonio rang six times and finally Dudley answered.

"What are you doing?" she said.

"Watching the boats on the lake. Waiting for you. Are you coming down? You want to go or not?"

"I want to go. Call Saint John."

"I already called him. He's free. Gayleen's up in Boston, as you noted. When do you want to go?"

"Right away."

"How about the fourth of July?"

"I'll be there. Where do I fly to?"

"Fly to San Antonio. We'll drive down. There's a hunting lodge down there I need to visit anyway. A hacienda. We can stay there for free."

"How hot is it?"

"No worse than where you are."

"I'm sorry I've been so mean to you the last few years."

"It's okay."

"No, it was mean as shit. I'll make it up to you."

"Let me know when you get a flight."

"A wasp bit me."

"You know what Kurt Vonnegut said about nature, don't you?"

"No, what did he say?"

"He said anybody who thinks nature is on their side doesn't need any enemies."

"I miss you, Dudley. You know that?"

"You know what a wedding ring is, don't you?"

"No. What?"

"A blow job repellent."

"Jesus," Rhoda answered.

"You know what the four most feared words in the United States are, don't you?"

"No. What?"

"I is your president."

"Jesus. Listen, I'm coming. I'll be there."

"I'll call Saint John. He'll be glad."

Rhoda hung up the phone, lay back against the satin pillow. My rubbish heap of a heart, she decided. I'm regressing. Well, they are my oldest compadres. Besides, where else will I find two men my own age who are that good-looking and that well-preserved and that brave? Where else will I find anybody to go to Mexico with in the middle of the summer? My ex-husbands are all snuggled down with their wifelets on little trips to Europe. Thank God I'm not sitting somewhere in a hotel room in London with someone I'm married to. About to make love to someone I've fucked a thousand times.

Well, I wouldn't mind having one of my old husbands here this afternoon. Yes, I must face it, I have painted myself into a corner where my sex life is concerned. I should get up and get dressed and do something with my hair and go downtown and find a new lover but I have run out of hope in that department. I don't even know what I would want to find. No, it's better to call the travel agent and go off with my brother and my cousin. Mexico it is, then. As Dudley always says, why not, or else, whatever.

Rhoda slept for a while, resigned or else content. When she woke she called Saint John at his office in New Orleans and they made their plans. Rhoda would fly to New Orleans and meet Saint John and they would go together to San Antonio and pick up Dudley and the three of them would drive down into Mexico. She would leave on July second. A week away.

During the week Rhoda's wasp sting got better. So did her mood. She dyed her hair a lighter blond and bought some new clothes and early on the morning of July second she boarded a plane and flew down to New Orleans. She took a taxi into town and was delivered to Saint John's office on Prytania Street. A secretary came out and took her bags and paid the taxi and Saint John embraced her and introduced her to his nurses. Then a driver brought Saint John's car around from the garage. A brand-new baby blue BMW convertible with pale leather seats and an off-white canvas top. "Let's take the top down," Saint John said. "You aren't worried about your hair, are you?"

"Of course not," Rhoda said. "This old hair. I've been bored to death, Saint John. Take that top down. Let's go and have some fun."

"We'll go to lunch," he said. "The plane doesn't leave until four."

"Great. Let's go."

They drove down Prytania to Camp Street, then over to Magazine and across Canal and down into the hot sweaty Latin air of the French Quarter. Tourists strolled along like divers walking underwater. Natives lounged in doorways. Cars moved sluggishly on the narrow cobblestone streets. Saint John's convertible came to a standstill on the corner of Royal and Dumaine, across the street from the old courthouse where one of Rhoda's lovers had written films for the Wildlife and Fisheries Commission. "Do you ever hear from Mims Waterson?" she asked.

"No," Saint John said. "I think he went back to North Carolina."

"If I hear North Carolina I think of Anna." They hung their heads, mourning their famous cousin.

"Anna," Saint John said, and moved the car a few feet farther down the street. "She was a strange one."

"Not strange, just different from us. Gifted. Talented, and besides, her father was mean to her. Her death taught me something."

"And what was that?"

"To be happy while I'm here. To love life. Tolstoy said to love life. He said it was the hardest thing to do and the most important. He said life was God and to love life was to love God."

"I don't know about all that." Saint John was a good Episcopalian. It bothered him when his cousins said things like that. He wasn't sure it was good to say that God was life. God was God, and if you started fucking around with that idea there wouldn't be any moral order or law.

"I thought we'd go to Galatoire's," he said. "Will that be all right?"

"That's perfect. Stop in the Royal Orleans and let me work on my face, will you? I can't go letting anyone in this town think I let myself go. I might have to come down here and scarf up a new husband if something doesn't happen soon with my life."

"What have you been doing?"

"Writing a travel book. Anna's agent is handling it for me. It might make me some money. At least pay my bills and get me out of debt."

"Will you write about this trip? About Mexico?"

"If there's anything I can use. Okay, there's the garage and they have space. Go on, Saint John, turn in there." He pulled into the parking lot of the Royal Orleans Hotel. The hotel was filled with memories for both of them. Secret meetings, love affairs, drunken lunches at Antoine's and Arnaud's and Brennan's. Once Rhoda had spent the night in the hotel with a British engineer she met at a Mardi Gras parade. Another time Saint John had had to come there to rescue her when she ran away from her husband at a ball. He had found her in a suite of rooms with one of her husband's partner's wives and a movie star from Jackson, Mississippi. Rhoda had decided the partner's wife should run off with the movie star.

"The wild glorious days of the Royal Orleans," Rhoda said now. "We have had some fun in this hotel."

"We have gotten in some trouble," Saint John answered.

"What trouble did you ever get in? You weren't even married."

"I was in medical school. That was worse. I was studying for my boards the night you had that movie star down here."

"I'm sorry," Rhoda said, and touched his sleeve. Then she abandoned him in the hotel lobby and disappeared into the ladies' lounge. When she reappeared she had pulled her hair back into a chignon, added rouge and lipstick, tied a long peach and blue scarf in a double knot around her neck, and replaced the small earrings she had been wearing with large circles of real gold.

"How do I look?" she asked.

"Wonderful," Saint John said. "Let's go." She took his arm and they walked down Royal Street to Bourbon and over to Galatoire's. Their cousin Bunky Biggs was standing outside the restaurant with two of his law partners. "Saint John," he called out. "Cousin Rhoda, what are you doing in town?"

"She's taking me to Mexico," Saint John said. "With Dudley."

"Oh, my Lord," Bunky said. "That will be a trip. I wish I was going."

"He's taking me," Rhoda said, very softly. It was all working beautifully, the universe was cooperating for a change. Now it would be all over New Orleans that she and Saint John were off on a glorious adventure. Bunky could be depended upon to spread the word.

"What are you going to do down there?" Bunky said. "There's no hunting this time of year."

"We're going to see some animals," Saint John said. "To have some fun." He was saved from further explanation. At that moment a delivery truck pulled up across the street and a tall black man emerged from the back of the truck carrying a huge silver fish. The man was six and a half feet tall. He hoisted the fish in his arms and carried it across the narrow crowded street. A small Japanese car squeaked to a stop. An older black man wearing a tall white hat opened a door and held it open and the fish and its bearer disappeared into the wall. We live in symbiosis with this mystery, Rhoda thought. No one understands it. Everything we think we know is wrong. Except their beauty. They are beautiful and we know it and I think they know it but I am far away from it now and get tired of trying to figure it out. Forget it.

The maitre d' appeared and escorted them inside.

The restaurant was crowded with people. The Friday afternoon professional crowd was out in force. Women Rhoda had known years before were seated at tables near the door, the same tables they might have occupied on the day she left town with the poet. People waved, waiters moved between the crowded tables carrying fabulous crabmeat salads and trout meunière and trout amandine and pompano en papillete and oysters Bienville and oysters Rockefeller and turtle soup and fettucini and martinis and whiskey sours and beautiful French desserts and bread pudding and flán.

"I should never have left," Rhoda exclaimed. "God, I miss this town."

Two hours later they emerged from Galatoire's and found the blue convertible and began to drive out to the airport.

"Dudley's been looking forward to this," Saint John said. "I hope we don't miss that plane."

"If we do there'll be another one along."

"But he might be disappointed."

"What a strange thing to say."

"Why is that? Everyone gets disappointed, Rhoda. Nothing happens like we want it to. Like we think it will."

"Bullshit," Rhoda said. "You're getting soft in the head, Saint John. Drive the car. Get us there. You're as rich as Croesus. What do you have to worry about? And take off that goddamn seat belt." She reached behind her and undid her own and Saint John gunned the little car and began to drive recklessly in and out of the lanes of traffic. This satisfied some deep need in Rhoda and she sat back in the seat and watched in the rearview mirror for the cops.

The plane ride was less exciting. They settled into their seats and promptly fell asleep until the flight got to Houston. They changed planes and fell back asleep.

Rhoda woke up just before the plane began its descent into San Antonio. She was leaning against the sleeve of Saint John's summer jacket. My grandmother's oldest grandson, she thought. How alike we are, how our bodies are shaped the same, our arms and legs and hands and the bones of our faces and the shape of our heads. Apples from the same tree, how strange that one little grandmother put such a mark on us. I was dreaming of her, after she was widowed, after our grandfather was dead and her hair would stray out from underneath its net and she gave up corsets. Her corsets slipped to the floor of her closet and were replaced by shapeless summer dresses, so soft, she was so soft she seemed to have no bones. Her lovely little legs. "Tell me again the definition of tragedy, I always forget." In my dream she was standing on the porch at Esperanza watching us play in the rain. We were running all over the front lawn and under the rainspouts, barefooted, in our underpants, with the rain pelting down, straight cold gray rain of Delta summers, wonderful rain. How burning we were in the cold rain, burning and hot, how like a force, powerful and wild, and Dan-Dan standing on the porch watching us, worrying, so we were free to burn with purpose in the rain. In the dream she is calling Dudley to come inside. Saint John and Floyd and I may run in the rain and Pop and Ted and Al but Dudley must come in. She holds out a towel to wrap him in. He was the sickly one, the one who had barely escaped with his life, three times, whooping cough and malaria and polio. And yet, he was stronger than we were. He was stronger than Saint John, stronger than Bunky Biggs, stronger than Phelan even. How could being sick and almost dying make you strong? Gunther told me once but I have forgotten. It was about being eaten and fighting, thinking you are being eaten and becoming impenetrable. Anna seemed impenetrable too but she turned out not to be. Rhoda shook off the thought. She got up very gingerly so as not to wake Saint John, and wandered down the aisle to the tiny bathroom to repair her makeup. She went inside and closed and locked the door. She peered into the mirror, took out her lipstick brush and began to apply a light peach-colored lipstick to her lips. A sign was flashing telling her to return to her seat but she ignored it. She added another layer of lipstick to her bottom lip and began on her upper one. How did being sick when he was little make Dudley so powerful? What had Gunther said? It was some complicated psychological train of thought. Because a small child can imagine himself being consumed, eaten, burned up by fever, overwhelmed by germs, taken, as children were taken all the time before the invention of penicillin and streptomycin and corticosteroids. Before we had those medicines children died all the time. So Dudley must have lain in bed all those terrible winters and summers with Momma and Doctor Finley holding his hand and waged battle because they begged him to live, because they sat with him unfailingly and held his hand and gave him cool cloths for his head and sips of water from small beautiful cups and shored him up, because they won, because he won and did not die, he became immortal. Nothing could eat him, nothing could make him die.

Rhoda blotted the lipstick on a paper towel. So, naturally, he likes soft-spoken blond women who hold his hand and he likes to take small sips of things from beautiful cups and he likes to hang out with physicians. He is always going somewhere to meet Saint John, they have hunted the whole world together. It is all too wonderful and strange, Rhoda decided, I could think about it all day. It's a good thing I don't live near them, I would never think of anything else.

She put the lipstick away and took out a blusher and began to color her cheeks. The plane was descending. The sign was flashing. He loves the battle, Gunther had said. And he thinks he will always win.

"He never gets sick," Rhoda had said. "They were jaguar hunting in Brazil and three people died from some water they drank and Dudley didn't even get sick. Everyone got sick but Dudley."

"He can't lose," Gunther said. "Because your mother held his hand."

"Sometimes they lose," Rhoda said. "My grandmother lost a child."

"But Dudley didn't lose."

"He thinks he is a god."

"What about you, Rhoda? Do you think you are a god?"

"No, I am a human being and I need other human beings and that is what you are trying to teach me, isn't it?"

"I don't have any plans for you."

"So you say."

Rhoda finished her makeup and returned to her seat just as the stewardess was coming to look for her. "I'm sorry," she said, and slipped into the seat beside her cousin. He was shaking the sleep from his head. "We slept too long," he said. "We must have drunk too much at lunch. Don't know what's wrong with me." He squinched his eyes together, squirmed around. "It's okay," Rhoda said.

"Where have you been?"

"I was in the restroom. I figured out Dudley. Want to hear?"

"Sure. Put on your seat belt."

"He has to kill or be killed."

"What does that mean?"

"He hunts to keep from dying because he was sick when he was a child."

"Rhoda." He gave her his bedside look. Indulgent, skeptical, maddeningly patronizing.

"Never mind," she said. "I know you don't like psychiatry."

"Well, I'm not sure it applies to Dudley." Rhoda gave up, began to leaf through an airplane magazine. Outside the window the beautiful neighborhoods of San Antonio came into view, swimming pools and garages and streets and trees and trucks, an electric station, a lake. The modern world, Rhoda decided, and I'm still here.

Dudley was waiting for them, standing against a wall, wearing a white shirt and light-colored slacks, beaming at them, happy they were there. They linked arms and began to walk out through the airport, glad to be together, excited to be together, feeling powerful and alive.

They stopped at several bars to meet people Dudley knew and danced at one place for an hour and then drove in the gathering dark out to the lake where Dudley's house sat on its lawns, filled with furniture and trophies and mementos of his hunts and marriages. Photographs of his children and his wives covered the walls, mixed with photographs of hunts in India and France and Canada and the Bighorn Mountains of Wyoming and Africa and Canada and Tennessee. Rugs made from bears were everywhere. Four rhinoceros heads were on one wall. Jaguar, tigers, lions, cougars, mountain sheep. He should have been a biologist, Rhoda thought. He wouldn't have needed so much room to hang the trophies on.

They cooked steaks on a patio beside the lake and ate dinner and drank wine and played old fifties music on the stereo and went to bed at twelve. Rhoda had an air-conditioned room on the second floor with a huge bearskin rug on the floor and a leopard on the wall. She cleaned her face and brushed her teeth and put on a gown and fell asleep. At three in the morning she woke. Most of the lights in the house were still on. She wandered out onto the sleeping porch and there were Dudley and Saint John, stretched out on small white enamel beds with a ceiling fan turning lazily above them, their long legs extended from the beds. If I had one chromosome more, she decided. One Y chromosome and I'd be out here on this hot sleeping porch in my underpants instead of in an air-conditioned room in a blue silk dressing gown. I'm glad I am a girl. I really am. They are not as civilized as I am, not as orderly or perfect. She turned off the lights they had left on and went back into her room and brushed her teeth some more and returned to bed. She fell into a dreamless sleep, orderly, perfect, civilized.

When she woke Dudley was in the kitchen making breakfast. "You ready to go to Mexico?" he asked. He handed her a tortilla filled with scrambled eggs and peppers. "Did you bring your passport?"

"No, I didn't think I needed it."

"You don't. It's all right. Well, we'll get off by noon I hope. I have to make some phone calls."

"Where exactly are we going, Dudley?"

"To see a man about a dog." They looked at each other and giggled. It was the thing their father said when their mother asked him where he was going.

"Okay," Rhoda said. "When do we leave?"

It was afternoon before they got away. They were taking a blue Mercedes station wagon. Rhoda kept going out and adding another bottle of water to the supplies.

"How much water are you going to need?" Saint John asked. "We'll only be there a few days."

"We can throw away any we don't want," she answered. "But I'm not coming home with amoebic dysentery."

"Take all you want," Dudley answered. "Just leave room for a suitcase and the guns."

"Guns?"

"Presents for Don Jorge. You will like him, Shorty. Well, Saint John, are we ready?" They were standing beside the station wagon. Saint John handed him the small suitcase that contained their clothes. In a strange little moment of companionship they had decided to pack in one suitcase for the trip. Dudley had pulled a dark leather case from a closet and each of them had chosen a small stack of clothes and put them in. They stuck the suitcase in the space between the bottles of water. Dudley put the gun cases on top of the suitcase. They looked at one another. "Let's go," they said.

"You got the magical-gagical compound?" Saint John asked, as they pulled out of the driveway.

"In the glove compartment," Dudley answered. Saint John reached down into the box and brought out a little leather-covered bottle that had come from Spain the first time the two men went there to shoot doves, when Saint John was twenty-nine and Dudley was twenty-seven. Saint John held the bottle up for Rhoda to see. "The sacred tequila bottle," he said. Dudley smiled his twelve-year-old fort-building smile, his face as solemn as an ancient Egyptian priest. That's what the Egyptians did, Rhoda thought. Had strange bottles of elixir, went on mysterious expeditions and ritual hunts. The Egyptians must have been about twelve years old in the head, about Dudley and Saint John's age. Remember Gunther told me I was arrested at about fourteen. I don't think Saint John and Dudley even made it into puberty.

Saint John raised the little vial-shaped leather-covered bottle. He removed the top. Inside the leather was a very thin bottle of fragile Venetian glass. He took a sip, then passed the sacred bottle to Dudley.

"Exactly where are we going?" Rhoda asked. "I want to see a map." Saint John replaced the top on the sacred tequila bottle and restored it to its secret resting place in the glove compartment. Then he took out a map of Mexico and leaned into the back seat to show it to her. "Here," he said. "About a hundred and twenty miles below Laredo."

Then there was the all-night drive into Mexico. The black starless night, the flat fields stretching out to nowhere from the narrow asphalt road, the journey south, the songs they sang, the fathomless richness of the memories they did not speak of, all the summers of their lives together, their matching pairs of chromosomes, the bolts of blue and white striped seersucker that had become their summer playsuits, the ancient washing machine that had washed their clothes on the back porch at Esperanza, the hands that had bathed them, the wars and battles they had fought, the night the fathers beat the boys for stealing the horses to go into town to meet the girls from Deer Park Plantation, the weddings they were in, the funeral of their grandmother when they had all become so terribly shamefully disgustingly drunk, the people they had married and introduced into each other's lives, the dogs they had raised, the day Saint John came over to Rhoda's house to help her husband teach the Irish setters how to fuck, the first hippie love-in ever held in New Orleans, how they had gone to it together and climbed up a liveoak tree and taught the hippies how to hippie. Their adventures and miraculous escapes and all the years they had managed to ignore most of the rest of the world. The way they feared and adored and dreamed each other. The fathomless idiosyncrasies of the human heart. All of which perhaps explains why it took all night to go one hundred and eighty miles south of the place they left at three o'clock in the afternoon.

First they stopped at the border to get temporary visas, then searched for diesel for the Mercedes, then crossed the border, then parked the car, then they goofed around Nuevo Laredo driving Rhoda around the boundaries of Boys Town. Then they went to the Cadillac Bar for margaritas, then had dinner, then found the car.

It was black night when they left the border town of Nuevo Laredo and began to drive down into Mexico. "Why don't we spend the night here and go on in the morning?" Rhoda asked a dozen times. "Why drive into Mexico at night?"

"Nowhere to stop," Saint John and Dudley said, and kept on going, taking sips out of the sacred bottle, which seemed to hold an inexhaustible supply of tequila. Rhoda was curled up on the back seat using her raincoat for a pillow, trying to think zen thoughts and live the moment and seize the day and so forth. I could be getting laid, she kept thinking. If I had expended this much time and energy on finding a new boyfriend I could be somewhere right now getting laid. I could have called an old boyfriend. I could have called that good-looking pro scout I gave up because of the AIDS scare.

"We were the lucky ones," she said out loud. "We got to live our lives in between the invention of the birth control pill and the onslaught of sexually transmitted diseases. We lived in the best of times."

"Still do," Dudley said.

"There was syphilis," Saint John added.

"But we had penicillin for that," Rhoda answered. "I mean, there was nothing to fear for about twenty years. If someone wanted to sleep with me and I didn't want to, I apologized, for God's sake."

"That's changed?" Dudley asked.

"It changed for me," Rhoda said. "I'm scared to death to fuck anyone. I mean it. It just doesn't seem to be worth the effort. I guess if I fell in love I'd change my mind, but how can you fall in love if you never fuck anyone? I can't fall in love with someone who has never made me come."

"Her mouth hasn't changed," Saint John said. "Rhoda, do you talk like that in public?"

"In the big world? Is that what you're saying? You're such a prick, Saint John. I don't know why we let you run around with us. Why do we run around with him, Dudley?"

"I like him. He's my buddy." The men laughed and looked at each other and Saint John handed Dudley the tequila bottle and Dudley handed Saint John the salt. They poured the salt on their folded thumbs and licked it off. They shared a lime. They replaced the top and put the sacred tequila bottle away. Nothing had changed. Dudley and Saint John understood each other perfectly and Rhoda sort of understood them, but not quite. "Unless you are both just as dumb as fucking posts and there is nothing to understand."

"What's she saying now?"

"I said I want to drive if you are going to get drunk and I want you to stop the car and roll up the windows and let's sleep until it's light. I don't like driving down through this desolate country in the middle of the night. I thought we were going to some hacienda. No one told me I was going to have to spend the night in a car."

"We're going," Dudley said. "We'll be there in an hour."

"It's two o'clock in the morning and you've already been lost twice and I don't think you have the slightest idea where you're going."

"You want some tequila, sister?"

"No, I want to get some sleep."

"You stopped drinking too? You don't get laid and you don't get drunk, that's what you're telling me?"

"That's what I'm saying."

"Then why do you want to be alive?" Dudley shook his head. "Have some tequila, honey. We'll be where we want to be when we wake up tomorrow. You'll be glad, you'll see."

"Why baby her?" Saint John said. "If you give in to her, she'll bitch all week."

"Fuck you," Rhoda said. She sat up and straightened her skirt and blouse and arranged her legs very properly in front of her. He was right, what was she living for? "Hand me that tequila," she said. "Is there anything to mix it with?"

"Wasting away again in Margaritaville," Rhoda started singing. Dudley and Saint John joined in. They worked on country and western songs for a while, which are hard songs to sing, then moved into hymns and lyrics from the fifties and back into hymns and finally, because it was the fourth of July even if they were in Mexico, into God Bless America and oh, say can you see and oh, beautiful for spacious skies, for amber waves of grain.

"Wait till you see the maize fields in the daytime," Dudley said. "That's how they bait the pamplona blanco. Maize fields on one side and irrigation ditches on the other. The whitewings are moving this way, and Don Jorge Aquillar and Mariana have been buying up all the leases for miles around. We're going to have some hunting this fall. Right, Saint John?"

"Who are Don Jorge Aquillar and Mariana?" Rhoda asked.

"The people we're going to see," Saint John said. "Right, Dudley," he went on. "If enough birds come. I can't bring my friends down here if the birds are scanty."

"Jesus, you've gotten cynical," Rhoda said. "Why are you so negative about everything?"

"Why are you picking on me?"

"I don't know, because I'm sick of riding in this car."

"Have another drink," Dudley said. "We'll be there in

a little while. It isn't far now." He was right. They went another fifteen miles and began to approach the outskirts of a town. "Agualeguas, 1000 Habitantes," the sign said. They drove past small adobe buildings, then around a curving dirt road, then past a two-story building and a store and through a darkened neighborhood and went down a paved road and drove another three miles and came to a long brick wall covered with bougainvillea. A tall wrought-iron gate was in the middle of the wall with painted white wooden doves on either side of the lock. Attached to the dove on the right and fluttering in the breeze was an extra wing. Dudley stopped the car and got out and pulled the wing from the dove. It was a billet-doux. "Dearest Dudley," he read out loud. "I am waiting for you with a worried heart. Ring the bell and we will let you in. Love, Mariana."

So this is why we couldn't stay at a hotel in Laredo, Rhoda thought. So this is why we had to drive all night in the goddamn car. Because his new girlfriend is waiting. I should have known. Well, who cares, I signed on for this trip and this is what is happening. Who knows, maybe she has a brother.

Dudley rang the bell and a girl in a white skirt came running out of a building and began to fumble with the lock. Then the gates were open and servants appeared and took Rhoda's bags and led her to a room with beautiful red stone floors and windows that opened onto a patio. They set her bag on one of two small beds and brought her water and turned down the other bed. Rhoda took off her clothes and lay down upon the small wooden bed and went immediately to sleep. Outside the window she could hear Dudley and Saint John and Mariana laughing and talking and pouring drinks. They never stop, Rhoda thought. Fifty-six years old and still spreading seed. "This is Mariana," Dudley had said when he introduced the girl. "Isn't she beautiful, sister? Wouldn't she make great babies with me?"

When Rhoda woke she was in a hacienda in Agualeguas, Mexico. Bougainvillea, red tile roofs, a parrot in a cage, rusty red stone floors, a patio with a thatched roof and an oven the size of a cave, ancient walls, soft moist air, beside the oven a bar with wicker stools. Above the bar, cages of doves, paloma blanco and paloma triste, whitewings and mourning doves, very hot and still. I am still, Rhoda thought, this is stillness, this is zen. A dove mourned, then another and another. The doves woke me, Rhoda decided, or I might have slept all day. It seems I was supposed to come here. It is the still point of the turning earth, like the center, the way I felt one time when Malcolm and I sailed into an atoll in the Grenadines below Bequia and I said, This is the center of the earth, we must stay here forever. Well, we can anchor overnight, he answered, but in the morning we have to push on. No wonder I divorced him. Who could live with someone as work-drugged and insensitive as that. Mother-ridden and work-drugged. My last millionaire. Well, now I'm broke. But at least I'm happy this moment, this morning in this lovely still place with red tiles and thatch and the doves in cages and Saint John and Dudley asleep next door in case I need protection.

The stillness was broken by the sound of a Mexican man putting chlorine in the pool outside Rhoda's window. She dressed and went out onto the patio to watch. The pool was a beautiful bright blue. The man had put so much chlorine into it that the vapors rose like a cloud above the water. The birch trees beside the pool had turned yellow from the chlorine fumes. They were like yellow aspens, beautiful against the green shrubbery and the red flowers of the bougainvillea. Death is beautiful, Rhoda thought, as long as it isn't yours. She remembered something. A bullfight poster they had seen in Laredo advertising a bullfight in Monterrey. Let's go, she had said. I'm in the mood for a bullfight. Of course, the men had answered. They were amazed. When last they messed with Rhoda she had lectured them for hours about going to football games and eating meat.

Mariana came out from the thatched kitchen carrying a tray with coffee and two cups. Brown sugar and cream.

"Will you have coffee?" she asked.

"Con leche, por favor," Rhoda answered.

"What will you do today? Have they said?"

"We are to go see the fields. And maybe to a bullfight. There's some famous matador fighting in Monterrey."

"What's his name?"

"Guillarmo Perdigo."

"Oh, yes, with the Portuguese. They fight the bull from horseback. It's very exciting."

"Muy dificil?"

"Oh, yes."

"Your English is so good."

"I am from Acapulco. I just came here to help my uncle."

"Dudley said it would be a famous place soon. That everyone will be coming here."

"We hope it will come true. If the doves come. We have bought up all the leases. We will have a monopoly."

"And some fun?"

"Oh, yes. That too." Mariana smiled, poured the coffee, looked away.

"Maybe the shopping clubs will come," Rhoda said. She watched Mariana, hoping to make her smile. Dudley had told Rhoda that groups of women came down to meet the hunters in Brownsville and Laredo and McAllen. Busloads of women from Shreveport and Baton Rouge came to meet the hunters at the Cadillac Bar and the bars of the Hilton Hotel and the Holiday Inn. It had begun by chance. First the men started coming down to hunt the doves. Then a group of women happened to be shopping in the border towns the same week. There were the bars full of good-looking hunters from all over the United States. So the women went home and told their friends and soon busloads of bored housewives from all over the South were down in the border towns buying up all the Mexican wedding dresses and piñatas in the world and getting laid at night by the hunters.

"That would be nice," Mariana said. "Do you think I should wake your brother?"

"No. Let sleeping men lie, that's what I always say."

"He told me to wake him at ten so he'd have time to see the fields. Carlos is here to drive you."

"Then wake him up. As long as you don't make me do it."

"Excuse me then." Mariana got up and moved in the direction of the men's rooms. I can't tell if she's shacking up with him or not, Rhoda thought. How Spanish not to flaunt it one way or the other. Spanish women are so mysterious, soft, and beautiful. They make me feel like a barbarian. Well, I am a barbarian, but not today. Today I feel as sexy as a bougainvillea. Rhoda sat back. The sun shone down between the thatched roof and the pool. The servants moved around the kitchen fixing breakfast, the yellow leaves fell into the bright blue pool, the carved tray holding the white coffeepot sat upon the wrought-iron table. Rhoda drank the coffee and ate one of the hard rolls and in a while Mariana returned with melons and berries, and the chlorine in the pool rose to the trees and the breeze stirred in the bougainvillea. The still point of the turning world, Rhoda thought. And what of the bullfight? Of the carnage to come? Death in the afternoon. What would it be? Would she be able to watch? It was getting hotter. Rhoda was wearing a long white skirt and a green and white striped shirt tied around her waist. White sandals. She was feeling very sexy, enchanting and soft and sexy. She looked around. There was no one to appreciate it. I'll just think about it, she decided. It's beautiful here, very zen and sexy. This is a thousand times better than being at home in the summer, a lot better than being bored.

The servants brought more coffee. Mariana returned. Then Dudley appeared, buttoning his khaki safari shirt. Saint John was behind him, dressed in white duck pants and wearing a cap with a visor.

"Why the cap, Saint John?" Rhoda asked. "Not that I don't like it. I do, a lot."

"It's from the Recess Club's last outing." He took off the cap, handed it to her so she could see the design. It was a man and woman locked in an embrace. "A Rorschach test," he added.

"Fabulous," Rhoda said. "How amusing."

"Give me back my cap." He retrieved it and planted it firmly back on his head. He had decided to be adamant about his cap. Rhoda moved nearer to him and put her arm around his waist. Poor Saint John, she decided. He could never wear that cap in New Orleans. All the trouble he's had all his life over pussy, he ought to get to make a joke out of it when he's in Mexico. "I think you're the sexiest man your age I've ever seen in my life," she said out loud. "I bet the ladies you treat fantasize about you all day long."

"I hope not," he said, but he was pleased and looked to Dudley to save him from himself.

"I thought Saint John got in the business to do it in the examining room," Dudley said. "Saint John, do you do it in the examining room?"

"Only with the nurses," he said, and they laughed and were relieved.

A driver appeared and they all piled into a four-wheel-drive vehicle and headed out of town toward the maize fields where the whitewing doves were already arriving in small numbers. From July to October more and more would come. Flying from the orange-red tops of the maize plants across the road to the irrigation ditches and then into the bush. It was all there, everything they needed, water and food and cover. All I need, Rhoda was thinking. All any creature needs.

"It will be a great fall," Dudley said, and opened a bottle of wine and began to pour it into paper cups. "Paloma blanco bastante, right, Mariana? Right, Pablo?"

"We have a monopoly all along the river and the ditches," Mariana said, "And twenty-three rooms and three vehicles. Now if Dudley brings us hunters we are happy." She reached across the seat and touched his knee. I can learn from these women, Rhoda thought.

"A great fall," Dudley said again. "A great year." He

leaned out the window, admiring the maize and the doves flying back and forth across the road as the vehicle approached the trees.

"I think I'll come twice," Saint John said. "Once in August and once in September. Look at that maize, Dudley. This place is going to be spectacular. I've counted twenty whitewings since we passed the dam."

"This place is going to be dynamite," Dudley agreed.

"I hope we make some money," Mariana said. "Uncle Jorge has invested very much."

"I'm coming back too," Rhoda said. "I know how to shoot. Don't I, Dudley?"

"Tell us which ones are the paloma blanco," he answered. "Start practicing."

On the way back to the hacienda they stopped at a native market and bought fruit and packages of orange tortillas. The tortillas were such a beautiful shade of orange that Rhoda forgot her vow not to eat native food and began to gobble them up.

"They are also good with avocado on them," Mariana suggested. "I will find you some when we get home."

"I like them like this," Rhoda said, and brushed orange crumbs from her skirt.

"If you get lost we can find you by the crumbs," Saint John suggested. "Like Hansel and Gretel."

"If I get lost I'll be with some good-looking bullfighter who fell for my blond hair."

"Dyed blond," Saint John said.

"Sunbleached. Don't you remember, Saint John, my hair always turns blond in the summer."

"Rhoda, you never had blond hair in your life. Your hair was as red as Bess's mane, that's why we said you were adopted."

"Is she adopted?" Mariana asked.

"No," Dudley answered. "She is definitely not adopted."

It was after one o'clock when they got back to the hacienda. Time to get ready to leave for the bullfight.

"It starts at four-thirty," Rhoda said.

"They are always late," Mariana answered. "If we leave here by three we'll be there in time."

"Time for a siesta," Dudley said.

"Siesta time," Saint John echoed.

There was an hour to sleep. A dove mourned, then another, a breeze stirred an acacia tree outside the window, its delicate shadows fell across the bed and danced and moved. Dance of time, Rhoda thought, light so golden and clear, and Zeus came to her in a shower of gold, clear, dazzling, and clear. Rhoda curled up into a ball and slept on the small white bed. She had not felt so cared for since she was a child. No matter how much I hated them, she thought, they protected me. They would throw themselves between me and danger. Why, I do not know. Taught or inherent, they would do it. How spoiled I am, how spoiled such men have made me.

The bullfight was in Monterrey, a hundred and twenty kilometers to the south and west. Mariana sat up front with Dudley. Rhoda and Saint John rode in back. They drove along through the afternoon heat. Dudley had the air-conditioner going full blast. Mariana had a flower in her hair. They talked of the countryside and what it grew and Rhoda asked Mariana to tell them who she was.

"My father is Portuguese," she began. "This is not unusual in the towns of the coast. The Portuguese are seafarers. There were seven children in our family. I am the second oldest."

"I'm the second oldest," Rhoda said. "We're the oldest of all our cousins. We used to rule the rest of them. The rest of them were like our slaves."

"Why does she say things like that?" Saint John asked.

"Because that's how she thinks." Dudley handed Saint John the leather-covered tequila bottle. "Whatever she does, that's the best. If she was the youngest, she'd believe the youngest child had the highest I.Q. She's the queen, aren't you, Shorty?"

"We did rule them. You used to boss Bunky and his brothers all around and I used to boss Pop and Ted and Al. We used to stay all summer at our grandmother's house, Mariana. We had a wild time. I guess those summers were the best times of my life. There were all these children there. Because of that I always thought a big family must be a wonderful thing."

"Give Mariana some of our Dudley-Juice," Dudley said. "Give her some magical-gagical compound, cuz. She needs a drink."

"It was nice to have the others," Mariana said. "But we ran short of money."

"What did your father do?" Rhoda went on.

"He is a builder," Mariana answered. "A contractor. He helped build the Viceroy Hotel in Acapulco. He will come for the hunts. If you come back you will meet him."

"How old is he?"

"He is sixty. But he looks much younger. He is a young man."

"Let's sing," Dudley said. "How about this?" He reached for Mariana's hand, began to sing. "When Irish eyes are smiling, sure it's like a morn in spring." I wonder if that stuff works on young girls, Rhoda thought. I wonder if that old stuff gets him anywhere anymore. I mean, it's clear the child likes him, but it may be for his money. They used to like him for his basketball prowess. No, maybe it was always for money. Why did boys like me? Maybe that was only Daddy's money. Well, now I'm broke. No wonder I don't have any boyfriends and have to run around with my brother and my cousin. Rhoda, stop mindfucking. Love people that love you.

"I can't wait to see this bullfight," she said out loud. "I saw one on my second honeymoon but I was so drunk I can't remember anything about it except that my feet hurt from walking halfway across Mexico City in high heels."

"It's how she thinks," Saint John said. He took a drink from the tequila bottle and passed it to Dudley.

"How do you think?" Rhoda said. "What are your brilliant thought processes? Hand me that tequila bottle. Where is all the tequila coming from? When are you filling it up?"

"Doesn't have to be filled," Dudley said. "It's magical-gagical compound. Up, down, runaround, rebound."

They arrived in Monterrey at four-fifteen, parked the car and found a taxi and told the driver to take them to the Plaza de Toros.

"Lienzo Charros," Mariana told the driver. "Pronto."

"I do not think it is open," he answered. "I don't think they are there today."

"It said on the poster they would be there. Guillarmo Perdigo is fighting."

"We'll see." The driver shifted his cigar to the other side of his mouth and drove through a neighborhood filled with people. He went down a hill and turned sharply by a stone wall and came to a stop. They could hear the crowd and see the flags atop the walls of the compound.

"I can't believe we're here," Rhoda said. She got out of the taxi and stood waiting by a tree while Dudley paid the driver. Her sandals settled into the soft brown dirt beneath the tree. The dirt moved up onto her toes and covered the soles of the new white sandals. She was being taken, the earth of Mexico was making her its own. The taxi driver waved and stuck his arm out the window and the little party weaved its way down the incline toward a wooden ticket booth beside a gate. Rhoda was very excited, drawn into the ancient mystery and the ancient sacrifice, the bull dancers of Crete and Mycenae, the ancient hunters of France, the mystery of the hunt and ancient sacrifice, and something else, the mystery of Dudley and Saint John. What allowed Dudley to hunt a jaguar in the jungles of Brazil? What allowed Saint John to don his robe and gloves and walk into an operating room and open a woman's womb and take out a baby and then sew it all back up? What was the thing that these men shared that Rhoda did not share, could not share, had never shared. I could never cut the grasshoppers open, she remembered, but Saint John could. I could pour chloroform on them. Poison, a woman's weapon since the dawn of time. But not the knife. The knife is not a woman's tool. She shuddered. Women give life. Men take it. And the species lives, the species goes on, the species covers the planet.

She took a twenty-dollar bill out of her pocket and

tried to buy the tickets but Dudley pushed her hand away and gave the ticket seller a handful of thousand-peso notes. Then they walked across a dirt enclosure to the entrance to the stands. Small boys played beneath the stands, chasing each other with toy pics, charging each other's outstretched arms. A blindfolded horse was led by, wearing padding and a double rein, a tall white Andalusian horse that looked quite mad. The excitement was very sexy, very intense. Four students wearing shirts that said Stanford University were in front of them on the stairs. They were drinking beer and laughing.

"These guys are just hairdressers," one student said. He was carrying a minicam video recorder.

"A high school football game," his companion added. Rhoda felt the urge to kill them. Rich spoiled brats, she decided. If they start filming this on that goddamn minicam, I'm going to throw up. How dare they come and bring that goddamn California bullshit to this place of mystery, this remnant of ancient sacrifice and mystery, this gentle culture and these lithe sexy Spanish men, how dare these California rich boys spoil this for me. She looked at Saint John and Dudley and was very proud suddenly of their intelligence and quietness. Dudley held the arm of the young Spanish girl. Both Dudley and Saint John spoke intelligible Spanish to anyone they met. We are civilized, Rhoda decided. We are polite enough to be here, to visit another world. But those goddamn muscle-bound California pricks. Who would bring a minicam to a bullfight? Fuck them. Don't let them ruin this. Well, they're ruining it.

They found seats and arranged themselves. Mariana on the outside, then Dudley, then Rhoda, then Saint

John. The music began, terrible wonderful music. Music that was about death, about sex and excitement and heat and passion and drama and blood and death. The music was about danger, sex was about danger, sex was the death of the self, the way men and women tried themselves against death. Ancient, ancient, Rhoda thought. Oh, God, I'm so glad to be here. So glad to be somewhere that isn't ironed out. "Without death there is no carnival." A long boring life with no carnival. That's what I've come down to, that's what I've been settling for. And will settle for, will go right back to. Well, fuck safety and security and fuck the fucking boring life I've been leading. She put her hand on Saint John's arm. Reached over and patted her brother on the knee. "Thank you for bringing me here," she said. "Thank you for this."

"You want a Coke?" Dudley said. "Do you want a beer or anything? You want a hat?" He motioned to a vendor and the man came over and Dudley bought a black felt matador's hat with tassels for Mariana and tried to buy one for Rhoda but she refused his offer. "I don't wear funny hats," she said, then looked at Mariana. "You have to have black hair to wear that hat. On black hair it looks great." Mariana pushed the hat back from her head so that it hung down her back on its black plaited cord. Her gold earrings dangled about her shoulders. It was true. She did look nice in the hat.

A vendor passed before them carrying a huge basket full of candy and cigarettes and packages of M&M's and sunflower seeds. His wares were spread out like a flower opening. It was a beautiful and heavy load and he displayed it as an artist would. Over his shoulder Rhoda could see the Stanford students standing side by side in their muscle shirts rolling film on the minicam and she hated them with a terrible and renewed passion.

"This is a small corrida," Mariana said. "Three bulls, but the matadors are good. Especially Guillarmo. I have seen him fight. He fought last year in Mexico City. And the last matador is Portuguese. Yes, you are lucky to get to see this. This is unusual for Monterrey."

"Como se dice in Español, lucky?" Rhoda asked. "No recuerdo."

"Fortunata," Dudley answered. "Bendecire and fortunata."

The music stopped for a moment and the vendor passed by again, this time carrying Cokes and beer in aluminum buckets. He was assisted by two small boys who looked like twins. "Gemelos?" Rhoda asked, and added. "Are they yours?" The vendor laughed and shook his head. He opened a Coke for Rhoda and one for Mariana and beer for the men. The minicam crew from Stanford had turned the camera Rhoda's way. She held up her hand before her face and waved them away. They kept on filming. "Tell them not to do that to me," she said to Saint John. "I mean it." Saint John waved politely to the young men and they turned the camera back toward the arena. Rhoda drank her Coke. The vendor and the twins moved on. The band picked up their instruments. They were wearing red wool jackets with gold buttons and gold trim. "They must be burning up in those uniforms," Rhoda said. She shook her head. They raised their tarnished brass instruments and the wild dangerous music began again.

"Look," Saint John said. "At the toriles, the bull pens, you can see the bulls." Rhoda looked to where he was pointing. She could see the top of a bull beyond a wooden wall, then the horns, then a second bull. They were very agitated. Very large, larger and more powerful and more agitated than she had imagined they would be. The blindfolded horse was led into an arena beside the toriles, a picador in an embroidered suit was sitting on the horse, another leading it. A bull charged a wooden wall, then disappeared out of sight. The door to the arena containing the blindfolded Andalusian horse was open now. The bailiff came in. He was wearing a tarnished gold uniform, riding a tall black horse with a plaited mane. Other men on horseback joined him. The paseo de cuadrillas was forming. Three small boys chased each other with paper pics across the barrera. "We could sit down there," Mariana said, "if you don't mind getting blood on your clothes."

Dudley and Saint John didn't answer. They were getting serious now, the homage athletes pay each other. "The seats near the arena are barrera," Mariana added, addressing her remarks to Rhoda. "The torero's women sit there." The women exchanged a look. In the bull pen a bull broke away from its keepers. There was a rush to corner it. Rhoda thought of Ferdinand, the old story of the bull that wouldn't fight. My sweet little mother, she thought, trying to deny all mystery and death for me. Except for the soft passing of Jesus into heaven, she would shield me from all older worlds.

But there are no Ferdinands, put out to pasture if they will not fight. The ones that won't fight go to the slaughterhouse. My sweet mother, smelling of talcum powder and perfume, reading to me of Ferdinand smelling the flowers. Then she would get up and go into the kitchen and cut the skin from a lamb, as happy as

Saint John in the operating room. Contradictions, half-truths. But this is true. Death in the afternoon is real danger, real death.

One of the toreros came up the stairs toward where they were sitting. He stopped in the barrera and spoke to a group of men. Two men stood up and embraced him. They are his father and his brother, Rhoda decided. The torero was tall, and lithe, like a dancer. Beneath his white shirt his skin seemed soft and white. Rhoda wanted to reach out and touch him, to wish him luck.

He sat down between the men he had embraced. The one who appeared to be his brother put an arm around his shoulder. They talked for a while. Then the torero got up as swiftly as he had arrived and left and went back down the stairs. The music grew louder, rose to a crescendo, descended, then rose again. The gates to the arena opened. The alguaciles rode out in his tarnished suit, leading the paseo de cuadrillas. Then the matadors, the banderilleros, the picadors. The mayor threw down the key to the toril. The matador who had come into the stand was wearing a short black jacket now, a montera, a dress cape.

The procession filed back through the gate. The gate to the toril was opened and the bull ran out. The matador, Guillarmo Perdigo, walked out into the arena and the ceremony began. This was no hairdresser, no high school football game, this was the most exquisite and ancient ceremony Rhoda had ever seen. The matador spread his cape upon the ground, squared his shoulders, planted his feet. The bull charged across the arena. The matador executed a pass, then another, then turned and walked away, dragging his cape. The bull pawed the ground, was confused, walked away. The matador turned to face the bull again, spread out his cloak, called to the bull. The bull charged again, and then again. The matador passed the bull's horns so close to his body, to his balls, to his dick. Rhoda held her breath. It's amazing, Rhoda thought. Where have I been while this was going on?

Dudley and Saint John had not moved. Mariana was still. A second matador appeared. Then the third. The matadors each did a series of passes, then the picadors came out on horseback and stuck the pics into the shoulder muscles of the bull. Rhoda was sickened by the sight. Fascinated and repelled, afraid for the matador and trying to hate the bull, but there was no way to hate him now since he was outnumbered. She turned her eyes from the bull's wounds, turned back to the matador who was alone with the bull again. This is so sexy, so seductive, she was thinking, the hips on that man, the softness of his face, of the skin beneath his white shirt. How many years has he worked to learn this strange art or skill? To allow that bull to move its horns so close to his hips, to his dick, then to turn his back and walk away. Still, to torture the bull. Rhoda, don't fall for this meanness. It is mean. Still, it doesn't matter, not really, not in the scheme of things. It is how things are, how things have always been. Men learned these skills to protect themselves from animals, to protect their children and their women. And it's so sexy, so fucking wonderful and sexy. I would fuck that bullfighter in a second, AIDS scare or not. I bet they think everyone from the United States has it. I bet no one in a foreign country would fuck an American now. They probably wouldn't fuck an American for all the money in the world. Rhoda leaned into the arena. The matador spread out his cape and made four beautiful and perfect passes, then drew the cape behind him and turned his back to the bull and walked away. He walked over to the barrio and was handed an older, redder cape and a sword. He came back out into the arena and displayed the sword against the cape and then prepared the cape for the kill. The bull looked confused, hesitant, worried. Perhaps he smelled his death. He walked away. "Toro," the matador called, "toro, toro, toro." The bull pawed the ground, made a fake pass, then moved back. The matador prepared again, spread out the red cape upon the ground, displayed the sword upon it, then moved the sword behind the cape, moved his feet very close together, then waited. The bull charged, the matador stuck the sword between the spinal column, planted it all the way to the hilt, and the bull's lungs filled with blood and it fell to its knees.

"The sword goes in and severs the spinal column," Saint John said. It was the first time he had spoken in thirty minutes. "It punctures the lungs and the lungs fill with blood. An easy death."

"Compared to what?" Rhoda said.

"Anything you can think of."

"What would be the easiest one?"

"Anna's wasn't bad. The shock of the freezing water would cushion the shock of the cyanide."

"What would be the easiest thing of all?"

"Fifty Demerols. I have a jar at home in case I have a stroke. I don't want to recover from a stroke."

"Nor I," Dudley said.

"Well, you probably won't have to," Rhoda said. "You'll just ruin your liver getting hepatitis down here

in Mexico and call me up and ask me to give you one.
God, I hope I don't have to give you a liver."

"I hope so too."

"Kidney," Saint John put in. "They don't transplant
livers."

The picador ran out onto the dirt floor, took out a silver
dagger, delivered the coup de grace. The matador
stared at the bull, then turned his face to the sky and
walked back across the dirt arena. Rhoda rose to her
feet with the crowd. This is what theater was trying to
do, she decided. This is what plays aspire to but this is
real death, real catharsis, real combat and real battle,
and the thing I can not understand and my shrink can
not understand. This is not subject to Freudian analysis
because this is older than Freud and besides I am not a
German Jew. I am from a culture more deadly and cold
than even these Spanish people descended from Moors.
She looked at the face of her brother and the face of
her cousin. They were completely satisfied. She was
satisfied. The young men from California were still sitting. They had put their camera away. Even they knew
that something had happened. Later, Rhoda thought,
they will get drunk and blow it off. Whatever the
matador represents they will not allow it in. They are
future people, remaking the genes. No second-rate
Mexican bullfighter can impress them. Perhaps nothing
can impress them. They will just get on a talk show and
explain it all away. They are the future, but I am not.
Rhoda stood up, extracted some dollar bills from her
purse, excused herself, and walked down through the
still cheering crowd toward the barrio. She wanted to be
near the matador, to breathe the air he breathed, to

experience the terrible sexiness of his skin, to look at him. She walked down the steps toward the concession stand underneath the stadium. He was standing with his back to her, his back was sweating underneath the soft white cotton of his shirt, his hair reminded her of a painting she had seen once of a Spanish child, so black it was no color, his neck was soft and tanned and the skin on his shoulders beneath his shirt seemed to her to be the sexiest thing she had ever seen in her life. He turned and handed something to a woman in a yellow blouse. Rhoda withdrew her eyes and walked on down the stairs and stood by a long concrete tub which held beer and Cokes. Two men were selling the drinks. "Un Coke," she said. "Por favor." The vendor extracted one from the depths of the icy water and removed the top with a church key. He handed it to her and took her dollar. The blindfolded horse stood against a fence. A few tourists walked toward the stand, two small boys chased each other with make-believe swords, the heat was all around her. She drank the cold sweet drink, felt her body melt into the heat. She stood there a long time. Finally the matador came out of a gate and walked toward two men in black suits who were awaiting him. The men embraced. The matador held one of the men for a long time. They were the same height and their arms slid around each other's shoulders. The black-suited man patted the matador's wet shoulder. The matador looked past his friend and saw Rhoda watching him. He met her eyes and received her tribute. I could fuck him, Rhoda thought. If I were still young enough to have hope, I would walk across this twenty feet of earth and hand him a paper with my name on it and tell

him where to find me. He would find me. He is young
and still has hope. She set the cold sweet Coca-Cola
down on the waist-high concrete tub and walked toward
the matador. He excused himself from the men and
came to meet her.

"Esta noche," she said. "Donde? Where will I find
you?"

"At the Inn of the Sun." His lips were as soft and full
as the skin on his shoulders. His hips were so close to
her. The smell of him was all around her.

"I will come there," she said. "When? At which hour?"

"A los siete. At seven." He reached out and took her
arm. "I was watching you. I knew you wished to speak
with me."

"I am called Rhoda. Se nombre Rhoda Katerina."

His fingers held her arm. "At seven," he said. "I will
wait for you." He moved closer. "Will you sit with me
now?"

"No, I am with my brother. I will come at seven." She
turned to walk back to the stairs. He walked with her to
the first landing. The tourists were watching them. The
men at the concession stand were watching them. The
children were watching them.

She walked back upstairs and rejoined Dudley and
Mariana and Saint John. The afternoon grew hotter.
Two more bulls were killed, including one from horseback. Then the corrida was finished. The band put up
their tarnished instruments and recorded music began
to play from the speakers. Rhoda and Dudley and
Mariana and Saint John went out on the street to find a
taxi but there was none so they began to walk toward the

hotel where they had left the car. I have to ask Mariana how to get to the inn, Rhoda thought. I have to get her alone and get her to help me.

"There is too much violence in the world," Saint John said. They were walking along the uphill dirt street, following the crowd in the direction of the town.

"Too much violence," Rhoda answered him. "What do you mean? You're as bad as those goddamn Stanford boys."

"You're all fascinated by your father's violence," Saint John said. "Look what it's done to Dudley."

"What are you talking about, Saint John? Make yourself clear. Jesus, it's hot as noon." They had walked out from the shade of the hill. It was as hot as noon, hotter, for the earth had had all day to soak up heat. Rhoda shuddered, thinking of the earth soaking up the blood of the bulls, blood soaking down into the earth and turning black. The matador's soft hands, the silver sword, the red cape and blood soaking down into the earth, the heat. I'm too old for him, Rhoda thought. But then, what difference would my age make? Remember when Malcolm gave that speech at the medical college and we went to the party with all the surgeons. The oldest man in the room was the most powerful. God knows how old he was, but he came across the room and took me. Just took me because he wanted me. And I allowed it. I left everyone else that I was talking to and followed him out onto the patio and he said, I want to take you somewhere tomorrow. Where was it he wanted me to go? To see a cadaver or something terrible or grim and Malcolm came and found me and brought me back inside because even Malcolm knew what was going on. So it has nothing to do with age or even violence although violence is one of its manifestations. It's power that matters, and in this Mexican town on this hot day power is killing bulls and Saint John knows it and is pissed off at the matador and pissed off at me.

"Goddamn, I wish we'd find a taxi," Saint John said. "I'm not sure this is the way to town."

"We can catch a bus," Mariana said. "If we go this way we will come to the main street and a bus will come by." They trudged up the dusty street and arrived at a main thoroughfare, and in a few minutes a dilapidated city bus picked them up and took them into town. She told them on the bus. First she told Saint John. "I'm going to meet the bullfighter," she said. "I'm going to his hotel."

"Of course you aren't," Dudley said. He turned around from the seat in front of her. "No, that's final."

"You don't tell me what to do. I don't take orders from you."

"He's right," Saint John said. "You can't go off with those people."

"Why not? Why can't I? What do I have to live for that's so important I'm supposed to be careful? My children are grown. I'm going to his hotel at seven o'clock tonight."

"You aren't going off with a Mexican bullfighter," Dudley said. "That is that. You aren't going to do that to us, Shorty."

"Is not a good idea," Mariana put in. "He would not really expect you to come even if you said you would. Not if he saw you were with men. He would think they would not let you." She lowered her eyes. "Even American men."

The bus had stopped at the downtown square. They filed off with the other passengers and found themselves in the middle of a parade which was forming to circle the square. A young girl in a red dancing dress was seated on a throne on a car. Her attendants were around her. A band was getting out its instruments.

"Be a good sport," Saint John said. "Don't start something with a matador. Not tonight, please, Rhoda." He took her arm. They began to walk toward the hotel where they had left the station wagon. "It was such a nice day. Why spoil it?"

"It's about death," Rhoda said. "I can't stand to do nothing constantly but displacement activities, amusements, ways to pass the time, until we get into the ground to stay. What's happening to us, Saint John? We are getting so old. We haven't got enough sense to be alive and it's almost over. We'll be crippling around with a pacemaker soon. We'll be completely dried out and ruined and I've never slept with a bullfighter in my life and I've always wanted to."

"Stop and get her a margarita," Dudley said. "Let's go in there." They had come to a restaurant on the square and went in and ordered a round of margaritas. They drank to the bullring and the brave matadors and Dudley began to give toasts.

"I'm going," Rhoda said. "I'm going over there at seven o'clock."

"Here's to the girl from the Delta, who never would say you are right, who never gives in, please give in, Rhoda, your brother and cousin are begging and begging you tonight." Dudley raised his margarita and signaled the bartender to bring them another round.

"Here's to the girls growing old," Rhoda raised her glass. She was into it now. "Who think they didn't get laid enough. Lost their youth and their puberty and their childbearing years being good for Daddy and big brother and fucking Jesus."

"Rhoda, you've had all kinds of husbands and boyfriends. What did you miss out on?"

"Normal relationships. Having one husband and loving him forever. Getting laid on a regular basis. Remember, Saint John, I missed from the time I was thirteen to nineteen. I never got laid during the great primitive fertile years, thanks to no birth control and our Victorian upbringing."

"So you want to go fuck some Mexican bullfighter in a cheap hotel to make up for not having a normal life?"

"Don't lawyer-talk me." Rhoda put down her margarita. She had decided to take it easy and not get drunk. "And you're not getting me drunk," she added. "So don't try that. It will just make me go over there more."

"He won't expect you to be there." Mariana reached out a hand and touched Rhoda's arm. This woman was so different from her brother. This woman was not careful. It would not be good to hunt with her.

"I want to go and fuck this guy. I'm fifty-three years old. It's none of anybody's business. I don't mess around with your sex lives."

"Hey, look," Dudley said. "Here come the musicians." Three guitarists had come in the door and were gathering around a table. The music began, beautiful, sexy, exciting music. A song Rhoda had heard once coming over a wall at a resort in Acapulco. "I heard that music in Alcapulco at Las Brisas once," she said. "I was having a terrible honeymoon with a man I didn't love. See, think of the terrible life I have been forced to live because I only liked power."

The music rose. Dudley motioned to the musicians to come their way. "I was on a honeymoon," Rhoda went on. "But all I did was get drunk and swim in this pool where you swam over to the bar. It was New Year's Eve and the musicians on the boats in the harbor played that wonderful music but it was all feet of clay, feet of clay." Rhoda finished the first margarita and started in on the second. The musicians came nearer. Dudley gave them money. "Let's dance, Shorty," he said. "I want to dance with my baby sister." Then the two of them went out onto the dance floor and began to dance together. My closest closest relative, Rhoda was thinking. My own big brother. My own hands and legs and arms and face. The gene pool, Jesus, what a fantastic mess.

"Que paso, mi hermano," she said. "We shall dance a little while and then go and see the bullfighter."

Dudley was a wonderful dancer and Rhoda loved to dance. He had Rhoda where he wanted her now and he knew it. They drank many margaritas and some wine and danced until the sun was far down below the horizon and seven o'clock had come and gone. "I have to go over to the Inn of the Sun," Rhoda kept saying. "What time is it?"

"Let me dance with her," Saint John said. "I never get to dance with Rhoda."

Sometime later they found a restaurant and ordered tortillas and frijoles and chili with mole verde sauce. They drank sangria and ate the wonderful gentle spicy food. "The food of a thousand colors," Rhoda said. "The food of orange tortillas and green avocado mashed and red peppers the color of the bull. I have to get over to the hotel, Dudley. I want to change clothes and go and see the matador."

"Let him wait," Saint John said. "The longer he waits the more he'll want you."

"You're just saying that," Rhoda said. But she was in a wonderful suggestive drunken state and so she began to picture herself as she had been at fifteen, sitting in her room for fifteen minutes while her date cooled his heels waiting for her to come down the stairs. Fifteen minutes, LeLe had always insisted. You have to make them wait at least fifteen minutes. Don't ever be on time. Don't ever be waiting for them.

When they had eaten all they could eat of the exotic dangerous food, they wandered back out onto the street where the parade had ended and the carnival had begun. There were street vendors selling food and musicians playing, children everywhere, young men and women walking in groups and couples, drinking beer and sangria and calling out greetings. Dudley and Saint John and Rhoda and Mariana walked back to the hotel where they had left the station wagon and took possession of the rooms Mariana's friends at the hotel had saved for them. There were two large adjoining rooms with big tiled bathrooms and a common sitting room. They carried their small amount of luggage up the stairs and went into the rooms and all fell down on one enormous walnut bed. Dudley was still making up limericks.

"There was a young girl from Brownsville, who always wanted to swill wine, and when they said no, she said, 'You know where to go,' and now she is there waiting for them."

"That's terrible," Saint John said.

"There was a young doctor from New Orleans, who always said, 'I am going to warn you, you'll get into trouble if you go out with me, for I won't marry you but I'll charm you.'"

"Worse."

"There was a young girl from the womb," Rhoda began. "Who barely got laid from there to the tomb. She said, 'Well, goddamn, so that's where I am, who did this to me. I must find a way to blame whom.' Sinking spell," she added. "I am having a sinking spell." She rolled up on the bed, cuddling into Saint John's shirt.

"Don't worry," he said. "It will pass."

A short while later Rhoda made a recovery. "Wait a minute," she said. "Where's my cosmetic kit? I have to do something about my face." She got up and found the small leather kit and carried it into the bathroom. She put the kit on the counter and examined herself in the dark mirror. I'll have to start all over, she decided. She took out a jar of Charles of the Ritz face cleanser and began to apply it to her face. Then she decided it was going to get all over her hair so she dug around in the bag until she found a shower cap and she put that on. She went back into the room and opened the suitcase and took out a clean blouse and disappeared back into the bathroom. Dudley had gone downstairs to procure a bottle of wine and some glasses. Saint John and Mariana were propped up on the bed having a conversation about whitewing dove hunting and how to get the birds to come to Laredo instead of Brownsville.

Now Rhoda decided to take a bath in the stone bathtub. She took off all her clothes and wrapped herself in a towel and took her clothes back out to the room and hung them over the back of a chair. "Don't mess these up," she said. "They're all I have to wear."

"He won't expect you to come," Mariana said, in a voice so low only Saint John could hear her.

"Don't talk about it," Saint John said. "Don't say anything. So tell me, how much land has your uncle leased? Has he got it all, all along the irrigation ditches?"

"Yes," she said. "Para ustedes solamente. All of it. All the land."

Rhoda ran water in the tub and washed the tub out. Then she filled the tub with hot water and got in. What was I going to do? she was thinking. Oh, yes, I'm going over there and see the matador. LeLe will have a fit. She'll die of jealousy. If Anna was alive what would Anna say? Anna would say, Rhoda, you are drunk. Rhoda giggled, the thought was very heavy, the thought would sink the hotel. That's why you got cancer, Anna, she decided. From always thinking shit like that just when I was about to have a good time. Rhoda examined her legs as they floated in the water. They didn't look very good anymore. There was something wrong with the quality of the flesh, with the color of the skin. I hate my fucking body, Rhoda decided. I just fucking hate growing old. There isn't one single thing about it that I like. She got out of the tub and wrapped the towel around her and went out into the room.

"We should give all our money to young people," she said. "It is wasted on people as old as we are."

"What's wrong now?" Saint John asked.

"The skin on my legs looks like shit. I mean, the flesh. The flesh looks terrible. There's something wrong with it. It's mottled looking. I hate myself. I hate getting old, Saint John, it sucks to hell and back."

Dudley came in the door with a tray. A Mexican boy

was behind him with the glasses. There was fruit and cheese and champagne and Dudley opened the champagne while the young boy tried not to notice that Rhoda was wearing a towel. She picked up her clothes from the chair and took them into the bathroom. Dudley brought her a glass of champagne and she drank it. Then she sat down at the bathroom stool and began to put on makeup.

Saint John turned on the radio beside the bed. Wild music began to play. United States music. It was a broadcast from Tom and Jerry's in Laredo. They were interviewing people who had come there to party all night. The music rose and fell and the people who were being interviewed told where they were from and what they had come to find in the border towns. It was funny. It was hilarious. The people were drunk and the broadcast was from Nuevo Laredo on the Mexican side so the interviewees were saying anything they wanted to say. It was amazing to hear people telling the truth on the radio. "I came down to get laid." "I came down to get drunk and let it all hang out." "I came down to find chicks." "I came down to find some guys to party with." "I came down to get away from it all." "It's cheap here." "You can find a party, you can have a good time." And so on.

Rhoda was getting back into a wonderful mood. The champagne had erased time. Her face was starting to look mysterious and beautiful. The bathroom was beautiful and mysterious. There were baskets of beautiful colored towels. There was a tile wall of fine blue and white figured tiles, each one different, each one made by hand. Everything in the room had been made by hand. The wicker stool was high and comfortable. The lights were soft. Rhoda applied more rouge, added some blue eye shadow, then a small single line of silver. She was beautiful, perhaps the most beautiful woman in the world. She thought of the matador pacing around the lobby of the hotel waiting for her. Waiting and waiting, thinking she wasn't going to come. Then she would appear. Fresh and lovely, his dream come true.

Dudley came into the bathroom and filled her champagne glass. He kissed her on the cheek. "I'm about ready to go," Rhoda said. "As soon as I finish my face."

"You're sure you want to go there?"

"I am sure. I have to have experiences, Dudley. I can't live my whole life in a straitjacket." She peered into the mirror, a deep line furrowed her brow. She was not quite as beautiful as she had been a moment before. "Don't back out on taking me. You said you'd take me. You promised me."

"I'll take you. We're going to see the matador. El matador." He was serious. He was playing the game. He wasn't making fun of her. One thing about Dudley, Rhoda decided. He never makes fun of me. Their eyes met. Yes, they were going to take the world seriously. Otherwise it wouldn't be worth ruling in case they were ruling it.

"What's going on in there?" Saint John called out. "I thought we were going to the Inn of the Sun God to see a matador. You better hurry up before I go to sleep instead."

"Let's go," Dudley said. "Come on if we're going."

It was eleven o'clock when they left the hotel and walked back to the square to look for the matador's inn. The fiesta was in full swing. The cafés were full. Mariachi music was playing. Music was coming out of the doors of the cafés. Drunks were falling off of benches on the square. People had been drinking all day. The car with the throne perched on top was parked sideways on a curb.

"Where is the Inn of the Sun?" Rhoda kept asking people.

"Keep going," someone said, "you will come to it."

"I'm just going over there," Rhoda kept saying. "I may not stay."

It was a square brick hotel on the corner of a street two blocks off the square. There was a lamp over a desk in the lobby. The light was dim and no one was behind the desk. They went into the lobby and waited. "Anybody here?" Rhoda called out. Dudley and Saint John didn't say a word. Mariana cuddled into Dudley's arm. A sleepy-looking man came out a door and asked what they wanted.

"I am looking for the torero, Guillarmo Perdigo," Rhoda said. "Is he staying here?"

"He was here," the proprietor said. "With his family. But he is gone now. He has been gone for a while."

"Will he be back?"

"I do not know. Perhaps in the morning. Perhaps not."

"Thank you," Rhoda said, and turned and led the way out of the inn and back out onto the street. They walked back to the hotel and went up to their rooms and told each other good night. Saint John was sleeping on a pull-out bed in the sitting room. After a while Rhoda got up and went into the room and got into the bed with him. "I'm lonely as shit," she said. "I want to be near you."

"Get in," he said. "It's okay. I love you. You're our little girl. Are you okay?" He reached over and pulled the cover up over her shoulder. He patted her shoulder. He patted her tired worn-out head. Her used-to-be-red, now sunbleached, hair which was not standing up very well under the trip to Mexico.

"No," she said. "I drank too much and besides I wanted to go and meet that bullfighter. I wasn't really going to sleep with him, Saint John, I just wanted to get to know him."

"But you might catch something, Rhoda. Kissing is worse than intercourse for some of the viruses. You should see what I see every day. It's really depressing."

"I never think of you getting depressed."

"Well, I do."

"I really wanted to go over there and meet him."

"We went there."

"No, you got me drunk to keep me from going."

"I was afraid for you, Rhoda. I love you." He patted her shoulder. He felt old suddenly, very old and far away from the world where he and Rhoda and Dudley had been alive and hot and terrible.

"I miss my children," Rhoda said. "I am lonesome for them."

"I know you are," Saint John said, and kept on patting until Rhoda settled down and was still.

"Thank God," he said out loud and moved his hand and went to sleep beside her.

In the morning they drove back to the hacienda. No one mentioned the matador or having gone to the inn to look for him. Rhoda folded her arms around herself and thought about the softness of his shoulders and his black eyes seeking out hers across the concrete concession stand. Win some, lose some, she was thinking. Outside the windows of the station wagon the hills were purple in the early light. I love this country, Rhoda decided. Any place that can produce a man like that is okay with me. Oh, God, I wish Anna were here. I could call up Anna and tell it to her and she would say, What a wonderful story. What a lovely encounter. Remember when she fell in love with that tennis player that summer in New Orleans and he fell in love with her? Some enchanted evening, only it was afternoon at the New Orleans Lawn Tennis Club right after they moved to the new club and the next day she showed up at my house at about eight in the morning so excited and horny and borrowed my makeup because she had been up all night making love to him in his apartment on Philip Street. God, what a summer. What a hot exciting world. It's true, we got to live in the best of times. Now they have to have rubbers and spermicides and be scared to death of catching things. We weren't afraid of anything. Oh, God, Guillarmo's back and arms are the most beautiful things I've ever seen in my life. I would like to see him fight bulls from now till the dawn of time.

"Rhoda?"

"Yes."

"Are you all right back there?" It was Dudley speaking. Saint John was asleep beside him in the front seat. Mariana was asleep beside Rhoda.

"Let's stop and get something to eat," Rhoda said. "I didn't have any breakfast."

"We'll be at the hacienda soon. Can you wait till then? I don't think there's anywhere to stop between here and there, except maybe a native market."

"No, it's all right. I forgot. I forgot where I am."

"I want to take you to a special place this afternoon. To meet some friends of mine."

"Sure."

"They're Americans who live down here. The man's from Austin and his wife is from Ireland. You'll like them. They have a really interesting place. An animal farm. You've never seen anything like it."

"Where do they get the bulls?"

"For the fights?"

"Yes."

"They raise them. It's quite an art, to keep the bloodlines pure and keep from overbreeding them. I'll take you sometime to one of the ranches where they are raised."

"I want to go back to Monterrey and see another bullfight."

"I bet you do."

"Okay, Dudley. Well, I'm going back to sleep." She closed her eyes. Went into a fantasy of meeting Guillarmo on an island off the coast of Spain. Having babies with him. Raising bulls.

They got back to the hacienda in Agualeguas at noon and had lunch and packed up and said their farewells to Mariana. Mariana was wearing a new gold bracelet with the teeth of a saber-toothed tiger embedded in the gold. Does he carry that stuff around with him in the glove compartment? Rhoda wondered. I mean, does he just have it ready in case he gets laid or does he go out at night and buy it? Maybe the fairies deliver it. God, what a man.

"I wish you could stay another night," Mariana said. "The rooms are free."

"We have to get back," Rhoda said. "Saint John and I

have to catch a plane tomorrow. Look, Mariana, could you get me a poster of that bullfight we saw yesterday? I mean if you see one or if you get a chance." Rhoda held out a twenty-dollar bill. "Keep this in case you see one and buy it and send it to me."

Mariana refused the money. "I'll send you one if I am able to find it." The women's eyes met. "Well, come back," Mariana added. She took Rhoda's hand. I love Mexico, Rhoda decided. I adore these people. I wish they'd all cross the border. This lovely tropic heat, the bougainvillea, Guillarmo's shoulders, blood on the arena floor.

"I'll come back," she said. "When the doves are here." Then Dudley embraced Mariana and Saint John embraced her and Rhoda embraced her and they got into the station wagon and drove off.

"One more thing we need to see," Dudley said, as he turned onto the asphalt road. "One more thing to show Shorty."

"What is that?" Rhoda asked.

"The cats," Saint John said. "Dudley wants you to see the cats."

It was two o'clock in the afternoon when they left the hacienda. They turned onto an asphalt road leading northwest to Hidalgo and Candela. A few miles outside of Candela they left the main road and followed the course of a stream until they came to a fence and a gate. Dudley stopped the car and got out and spoke into a microphone attached to the gate. In a few minutes a boy came on a bicycle and opened the gate with a combination and held it while they drove in.

A well-kept road made of crushed stone led uphill between acacia and scrub birch trees. Dudley drove the station wagon carefully up the road. The road grew steeper and he shifted into second gear. Rhoda was leaning up into the front seat now, trying not to ask questions. They had all slipped once again into their childhood roles. Dudley, the general and pathfinder. Saint John, the faithful quiet lieutenant. Rhoda, lucky to be there, lucky to get to go, interloper.

"You may see a lion along here," Dudley said. "Don't be surprised if you do. They get loose. Dave Hilleen and I had to shoot one last month. Hated to have to do it."

"A lion," Rhoda said. Very softly, very quietly. "He's kidding, isn't he, Saint John?"

"No, he's not," Saint John said. "You'll see."

The road wound down a small hill, then across a wooden bridge. The bridge covered a creek that crossed and recrossed the road.

"There's a springbok," Saint John said. "Oh, there's the herd." Rhoda looked and there beneath the trees was a herd of twenty or thirty African springbok. Their tall sculpted horns rose like lilies into the low hanging limbs of the scrub brush. They quivered, then disappeared like a school of fish.

"My God," Rhoda said. "How lovely. How divine."

"There are kudu and sheep and deer," Dudley said. "We're hoping to get some rhino in the fall."

"You're kidding."

"No, he's not," Saint John put in.

"They'll love it here," Dudley said. "It's exactly like parts of central Africa. Only safer and there is hay. It's conservation, Shorty. Someday, this may be the only place these creatures live. The African countries are destroying their herds. They're being hunted out and their preserves raped. They're beautiful, aren't they?"

"Do you hunt them?"

"Very little. We sell them to zoos. Sometimes we trade them for cats."

"All right. I'll bite. What cats?"

"You'll see," Saint John said. "Wait till you see."

"Cats the circuses can't train. Ones that go bad. The one Dave and I shot was an old lion that went bad. Ringling Brothers paid us to take him."

"Who does this belong to?" Rhoda asked. "Who pays for all of this?"

"It pays for itself. Dave paid five thousand to shoot the lion. He was scared to death. I didn't think he was going to pull the trigger when it charged. Jesus, I never saw a man get so white. Afterwards he said to me, I was scared to death, Dudley. How do you do that in the wild? Just like you did it here, I told him. It's him or you. It took him two shots." Dudley was talking to Saint John now. "One glanced off the ear and one went in an eye, ruined the head. I shot for the heart and lung when I saw his first shot miss. Old Dave. I never saw a man go so white."

"Who started all this?" Rhoda asked. "Who does this belong to?"

"These are nice folks here," Dudley said, suddenly stern. "They're friends of mine. Be nice to them and try not to talk too much."

"Of course," she said. "I'm always nice to everyone." Saint John sniggered, and Rhoda started to tell him to go fuck himself but for some reason she didn't feel like making Saint John or Dudley mad at her right that minute.

They had come to the top of a rise. A Caterpillar tractor with a grader blade was parked beside the road. Two

Mexican boys sat underneath an umbrella drinking from a stone jar.

A house was at the end of the road. An old stone house like something out of a nineteenth-century English novel. It was three stories high with turrets and a tower. In the field behind the house were structures that looked like huge greenhouses. They were tall cages, sixty feet wide by eighty feet long. There were three of them, at intervals of forty feet, constructed of steel bars three inches thick. Swings were suspended from the ceiling beams and some of the cats were sitting on the swings. A leopard, Rhoda thought. That's a leopard. And that's another one. She was struck dumb. Now she did not have to try to be quiet. Nothing could prepare you for this, she decided, no words could prepare anyone for this.

Dudley drove the car up to the house and parked it. Children appeared on the back porch. The caretaker's children. A tall girl, maybe twelve or thirteen, a boy a little older, a smaller girl, an even smaller boy. They were dark-skinned and dark-haired but did not look like Mexicans. "Are they Mexican?" Rhoda asked.

"Of course."

"They don't look it."

"Their mother is Italian. Where's your momma?" Dudley called out. He opened the door and got out. "Hand me that sack of rolls," he added. They had stopped at a bakery in Anahuac and bought sweet bread and raisin loaves for the children. Dudley handed the sack to the oldest girl. The boy smiled and held out an animal he was wearing on his arm. "Baby jaguar," the boy said. "They are all gone for the day, gone hunting with Redman."

"We just came by to see the cats," Dudley said. He patted the jaguar. He got back into the car. "We'll be back to the house. I want to show my sister the cats." Rhoda was half in and half out of the car. Now she got back in and shut the door.

"The momma killed the other one," the boy said. "We are raising this one on a bottle."

"We'll be back," Dudley said. He put the car in gear and backed out of the parking place. The children arranged themselves on the porch stairs, the boy held up the baby jaguar, flies buzzed around the porch and the car, the ground was dry and yellow. Rhoda sat on the edge of her seat. Behind them was a fourth cage. It was full of very large cheetahs, at least three cheetahs. "That cage isn't big enough for the cheetahs," Dudley said. "We have to do something about it. We didn't know we were going to have so many. The cougar need better cages, too. There are fourteen cougar now. Too many, but everyone keeps sending them and no one wants to hunt them."

"Embarrassment of riches," Saint John muttered. Dudley ignored him and drove the car from the driveway and out into the field where the cages rose like monuments in the hazy blue sky. We will get bogged down in the field, Rhoda thought. The car will stop and we'll have to get out. Why do the men in this family always have to drive cars into fields? Why do I always end up driving on a field or in a ditch? Why can't we stay on the road like other people? Don't talk. Don't say a goddamn word. If you object it will just make him do it more. You can't stop Dudley by telling him not to do something. Just be quiet and it will soon be over.

"How do you like it?" Dudley said, and laughed. He

began to circumnavigate the cages. Tigers were in the first one. At least five tigers, four gold and white striped tigers and one black tiger lounging on top of a concrete shelter. As they passed the cage Rhoda saw that a sixth tiger was inside the shelter, a huge black tiger twice as large as the others, taking up the coolest, most protected spot in the concrete shelter. She shuddered, tried to take it in. Dudley drove on. In the second cage were Bengal tigers, with faces as big as car windows. Three Bengal tigers sitting together on swings looking at her with their huge heads. In the third cage were lions. A lioness and three young cubs. Dudley drove down to a fourth cage, which could not be seen from the house. Jaguars were in that one. There were more cages in front of the house, protected by shrubbery and trees.

"What are in those?" she asked quietly.

"Leopards and cougar and some more lions," Dudley said. "We have three lionesses with cubs now and the ones in the pasture."

"What pasture?" But then she knew. Dudley had stopped the station wagon beside a flimsy-looking forty-foot-high fence. Inside the fence was a huge lion. Behind him in the tall grass were two lionesses with their cubs. The lion turned his head their way. Dudley rolled down the automatic windows and opened the sun roof. "Aren't they gorgeous, Shorty?" he said. "Aren't they something?"

"My God," she said. Dudley got out and walked over to the fence. "Hello, Waylon," he said. "Long time no see." The lion roared, a long deep rattling in the throat. Dudley turned his back to the lion and walked away.

"Don't worry, Shorty," he said. "He wants me but not badly enough to do anything about it today." Rhoda could hear him but she was only looking from the deepest part of the back seat. She had tried looking at the lion out the window but it was like staring over a precipice. Still, she could hear every word Dudley said, every sound of the world, suddenly she could hear every nuance, every blade of grass.

"Don't talk to him," she said. "Don't do anything else. Get back in the car." Dudley turned back to the lion.

"Get in the car," Rhoda called out. In a very soft voice. "Roll up those windows. Get in the car and get me out of here. Saint John, roll these windows up."

"The windows wouldn't stop him," Saint John said. "If he wanted to get in the car he could do it."

"Well, drive it then," Rhoda said. She called out the window in the loudest voice she could muster: "Dudley, get in the car. Get in this car and get me out of here. I don't like it. I don't like that lion. Or those cats. Get me out of here."

"I thought you were into violence now," Saint John said. "Bullfighters and blood and all that."

"Not when I'm part of the ring. Roll the windows up, Saint John, this is madness. That fence isn't big enough to stop a dog, much less a lion. Get Dudley back in the car. Let's get out of here. I don't like it here."

Dudley spoke to the lion again. "You want me, don't you, Waylon. Show Rhoda what you need." He turned his back to the lion again and began to walk away from the fence. The lion moved toward the fence.

"Oh, shit," Rhoda said. "I'm driving off, Dudley. I'm leaving you here. Roll those windows up, Saint John. Roll them up this minute, do you hear me?"

"It's okay," Saint John said. "You're okay."

"I am not okay. I am scared to death." Rhoda pulled

herself into a ball in the very middle of the back seat. She considered climbing into the trunk, but there was no trunk, it was a station wagon.

Dudley turned back to the lion. "Old Waylon," he said. "He hates me but he doesn't know why. You don't know why, do you, Waylon? Except you know I'm not afraid of you."

"Get in the car," Rhoda yelled. "Get in the car this very minute. Roll those windows up. Oh, God, why did I come down here to fucking Mexico in the middle of July. Have they closed the window yet? Please close the window, Saint John. Dudley, close the goddamn sun-roof and get back in the car and get me out of here. I have had all I can take of these goddamn terrifying unbelievable cats. I don't want to see them anymore. Take me to that house." He was still standing by the lion. "It's bad karma," Rhoda continued. "It's terrible karma to have these animals here. They should not be here. They should be dead or else back where they came from, where the Indians or Chinese or Africans or whatever can kill them themselves. If they lived where I lived I'd kill them all tonight. Get back in the car. Leave that lion alone." The lion bounded for the fence. Dudley laughed. Saint John got back in the car.

"Start the car," Rhoda said. "Saint John, start the car."

"Not yet. Go on up to the house if you're scared."

"Hell no."

"They can't get out, Rhoda. Oh, I guess the lion could get over the fence, but he doesn't really want to."

"Okay, I'm going. I can't take any more of this." Rhoda opened the car door. She looked toward the house. The children were standing on the stone steps holding the baby jaguar. "I'm going to the house," she said. "Fuck being out here with these goddamn lions." She stepped down on the grass, shut the car door, and began to run. "Don't get so excited," Dudley yelled. *Don't get them excited,* she thought he said.

"Watch out," Saint John called. "Watch your step." Rhoda sprinted toward the house, which seemed a mile away. She ran faster and stepped into a gopher hole and turned her ankle and went sprawling down across the dry yellow grass. Pain shot up her leg, then something was on top of her. It was Saint John. He knelt beside her and began to feel the bones in her foot. "Get me into the house," Rhoda was yelling. "Carry me into that house and lock the door."

Rhoda lay on a filthy horsehair sofa in the parlor of the stone house. One-half of the sofa was covered with the skin of a mountain sheep. Her broken foot lay propped on the sheepskin. By her side was a marble table with a statue of Mercury, wings on his feet. Saint John had gone into the kitchen to call the hospital in Laredo. Dudley was outside the window helping the young girls feed the jaguar. I am lying on this sofa catching ring-worm, Rhoda decided. The worms are going into my ankle through my wound and into the soles of my feet from where that dreadful little abandoned jaguar shit upon the floor. The children will have ringworm too. They will be bald and dead from the bad karma in the place. Live by the sword, die by the sword. There's no telling what will happen now. I don't even know if Saint John is a good doctor. Being my cousin doesn't make him good enough to set my foot, even if we do think our genes are superior to everyone else's in the whole fuck-ing world. "It hurts," she called out. Then yelled louder.

"My goddamn foot is killing me, Saint John. Please come give me something for my foot."

Dudley stuck his head in the open window. "What's wrong, Shorty? What's wrong now?"

"My foot is broken. And I want to go to the hospital. I don't want to wait another minute. It's your fault for not taking me to the house when I asked to go. I didn't know we were going to see these lions. Who said I wanted to go see a bunch of real lions? That fence wouldn't hold a lion for a minute if it wanted to get out. It could get out and kill everyone in the place."

"We're going in just a minute," Dudley said. "As soon as Saint John gets off the phone."

"Then hurry up," she said. "It's killing me. It's about to kill me, Dudley."

Saint John entered the room carrying a glass of water and a bottle of Demerol pills and stood by while she swallowed one. The water will give me amoebic dysentery, she decided. But I can't help that for now. "Where did the water come from?" she asked. "What kind of pills are these?"

Then the pain was better and finally stopped, or, at least, Rhoda didn't have to suffer it any longer. They carried her out to the station wagon and laid her out in the back seat beside a box of frozen pamplona blanco and two cases of German wine and the guns. Saint John borrowed an embroidered pillow from the children and arranged it underneath her head and propped her injured foot on a duffel bag and then Dudley made long elaborate farewells and they drove off down the line of caged animals. The panthers scurried around their cages. The lionesses flicked their tails. The lion cubs played with their paws. The Bengal tigers turned their stately faces toward the car like huge Indian sunflowers. The kudu pricked up their ears, they moved like leaves before the wind. The peacocks flew up to the fence posts. The Mexican guards waved and opened the gate. Dudley returned their wave and drove on through. Then he reached down into the glove box and took out the secret leather-covered tequila bottle and passed it to his cousin.

"When was the first time you two ever went hunting together?" Rhoda asked drowsily.

"When Saint John was ten and I was eight," Dudley answered. "Remember, Saint John, Uncle Jodie lent us his four ten and that little rifle, that twenty-two, and we went bird hunting, across the bayou behind the store."

"We were quail hunting," Saint John added. "We scared up a covey but we missed and then you shot a rabbit. Back where Man's cabin used to be."

"We skinned it and Babbie cooked it for us that night for dinner." They leaned toward each other in the front seat of the car, remembering.

"I took my old harpoon out of my dirty red bandanna," Saint John began singing. "And was blowing sweet while Bobby sang the blues."

"Blowing soft while Bobby sang the blues," Rhoda corrected sleepily from the back seat. "Not blowing sweet." She sank back down into the Demerol. The hunters looked at each other and shook their heads. A hawk high above them in the air spotted the car and was blinded by the reflection of the sunlight in his eyes.

"From the coal mines of Kentucky," Saint John started again. "To the California hills, Bobby shared the secrets of my soul."

*　　*　　*

A few days later Rhoda was back in her own house, safe from spotted fever and hookworm and amoebic dysentery and adventure. Her ankle was in a cast. She had a pair of rented crutches and a rented wheelchair. She had a young girl from the nursing school who was coming by in the mornings to fix her breakfast. She had an old boyfriend who taught history who was coming over in the afternoons to cheer her up. She had accepted an offer to teach Latin during the fall semester, replacing a young man who had gone crazy in the summer and run off to California without telling his department chairman. He had sent a note. "I can't bear their wretched little faces," the note said. "What do they need with Latin?"

The department chairman had called Rhoda and asked her if she could fill in. He had gotten her on the phone the day after Dudley had delivered her to her house. "Yes," she had said. "I will teach your class. I need some order in my life."

Now she sat in the wheelchair on the patio and watched the robins picking up seeds on the freshly mowed lawn. Her hands lay on her legs. She thought about her boring boyfriend. She thought about the sweet little nursing student who was fixing her such boring sweet little meals. She thought about lying in the back of the station wagon all the way home from Mexico and Saint John's hopeful, grating, off-tune voice singing the collected works of Kris Kristofferson and the collected works of Willie Nelson.

She thought of Dudley and how long they had all managed to live and how strange that they still loved each other. We know each other, she decided. Nothing has to be explained. No questions asked. *I wish them well.*

Even if they do think it is all right to fuck around with a bunch of lions and tigers and risk their lives and keep on hunting when it is the twentieth century and for a long time men have dreamed they could evolve into something less dangerous and messy and bloody. Still, there was that bullfight.

The sun came out from behind a cloud and flooded the patio. Rhoda sank deep into herself. Moved by the light.

She considered her boyfriend, who did good dependable useful work in the world and how boring and pointless it was to make love to him. With or without her foot in a cast she had no passion for the man. Her chin fell to her chest. We are not making progress, she decided. This is not progress.

I will go back with them in September. To kill the beautiful and awkward paloma blanco and pluck them and cook them and eat them. Anything is better than being passionless and bored. There's no telling who might be down there this fall. No telling what kind of gorgeous hunters might shut me up for a few hours or days and make me want to buy soft Mexican dresses with flounces and rickrack and skirts that sweep around my ankles. Bullfighters are waiting and blood on the arena floor. Blood of the bull and fast hot music and Mexico. "I should have left a long time ago," she began humming. Progress is possible, she decided. But it's very, very slow.

Several weeks later, when her ankle had healed enough that she could walk, she drove downtown to the travel agency to buy her ticket back to San Antonio. At the corner of Spring Street and Stoner she changed her mind and went to her old hippie psychiatrist's office instead. She parked the car and went in and asked the receptionist to make her an appointment. Then she went home and began to write letters. It was a cool day. The first cool day in months. The light was very clear. The trees were just beginning to turn their brilliant colors. Fall was coming to the mountains. Life was good after all. Peace was possible. Ideals were better than nothing, even if they were naïve. Here I go again, Rhoda thought, one hundred and eighty degrees a minute. She stuck some paper in the typewriter and began to write the first of the know-nothing letters. The proto-wisdom papers of the fall of 1988.

Dearest Dudley (the first letter began),

We have been the victims of Daddy's aggression all our lives. The pitiful little victims of his terrible desire for money and power. All he understands is power. He doesn't have the vaguest idea how to love anyone and neither do you and I. We must save ourselves, Dudley. Don't go back to Mexico and drink tequila and run around with lions. Come up here and visit me and we will sit on the porch and drink coffee and try to think of things to do that are substitutes for always being in danger. We could play cards. I will play cards with you for money, how about that? I don't know anything now. I don't know where to begin.

We need to talk and talk and talk. Please come.

Love, Rhoda

Dear Saint John,

Don't go back to Mexico and catch amoebic dysentery. Come up here instead. We don't need to kill things in order to eat. All we need to do is stay alive and work and try to appreciate life and have a good time.

Come on up. Dudley and I are going to revive card

games. We are going to play poker and drink a lot of coffee and I'll make biscuits for breakfast.

We'll have new times instead of old times.

Love, Rhoda

P.S. I'm sorry about that bullfighter. I really am.

P.P.S. I had this vision of the three of us huddled together on the floor at Esperanza sucking on each other for sustenance and love. Trying to get from each other what we couldn't get from the grown people. All those terrible years — our fathers at the war and our mothers scared to death and the Japs coming to stick bamboo splinters up our fingernails and you and me and Dudley trying to mother and father each other. Life is not easy for anyone. That's for sure. I don't think we really understand much yet and may be losing the little that we used to know. We don't need Mexico, old partner. We need something to hold on to in the dark and someone to remind us of where we really are. We are spinning in space on this tenuous planet. I won't let you forget that if you won't let me.

Love and love again, me.

Rhoda sealed the letters into envelopes and addressed them. Then she got into the car and drove down the hill and deposited them in the box at the post office. She was in a good mood. She even remembered to think it was miraculous that man had learned to write, not to mention invented a system to get letters from one place to another. Not to mention taming horses and fighting bulls and living to grow up. Every now and then someone grows up, she decided. I've heard about it. Why not, or else, whatever.